MW00945153

I Know Very Well
How I Got My Name

A Novella By Elliott DeLine

Copyright © Elliott DeLine, 2013

All Rights Reserved

Edited by Red Thomas

For more info, visit elliottdelineofficial.wordpress.com

AUTHOR'S NOTE: This novel is a work of fiction. Names, characters, places, and incidents are either products of the author's imagination or are used fictitiously. Any resemblance to actual persons, living or dead is, quite frankly, inevitable.

Cover art "Untitled Self Portrait" © Elliott DeLine circa 2006

Printed in the United States of America

This book would not have been possible without the generous donations of the following individuals:

Andy Molloy
Carolyn Tucker
Chelsea Brown
Curtis Myers
Cory Haughton
Dave Guitard
Donna Heltzman
Dottie Renehan
Graham Donelan
vegangraham.tumblr.com
Heather Datta
JD Haley
Kevin McClave
Linda Kirbow
Oliver Walker
RL

Thank you so much to those people listed above. In addition, thank you to all my supportive friends, on facebook, tumblr, and IRL who have supported me. Your encouragement has meant everything. In particular, thanks to Mark Simpson, Evelyn Deshane, Red Thomas, Gary Meader, TT Jaxx, Adrian Dae Tripper, Samael Bowen, Maura C. Smith (thischarmlessgirl), Bear Falcon, Geoff McClarney, Blake Chamberlain, K. Funk, A.J. Bryce, Meredith Richmond, George Allen, Minnie-Bruce Pratt, Michael O'Connor and his Fall 2012 Gender and Literary Texts class, my family (especially Aunt Linda), and everyone else who has made their support or enjoyment of my writing known.

Dedicated to my grandmother, Esther Elinor Connelly Renehan, who dreamt of becoming a writer.

1911—1996

ЄЖЗ

You think you were my first love
You think you were my first love, but you're wrong
You were the only one who's come and gone

-Morrissey, "I Know Very Well How I Got My Name"

Watch Out For Dragons

We drive to Grandma's house. It's a Tuesday afternoon in early spring—we always go on Tuesdays. My mom stopped to get us food at Burger King. This is another thing we only do on Tuesdays. She gets a Whopper, and I try a hamburger for the first time. It's okay.

Grandma lives in Eastwood, on the top of a large hill. First we must drive on the highway through the city, with the black smoke stacks and the steeples. Her address is 264 Clover Ridge Drive. The house is white with black shutters: an a-frame, with a pine tree on the right and a wood sign nailed to the house that reads CONNELLY —that's my mom and Grandma's last name. It has two shamrocks on either side because we are Irish.

It is a small house—about half the size of ours. It's funny, because my mom had four sisters. Seven people once lived at 264 Clover Ridge Drive: now it's only my grandma.

Grandma is excited to see us, but she understands that I don't like to be hugged and kissed. Instead, she smiles down at me and says she's so glad I'm here. She has short, gray hair feathering around her head, big glasses, and happy eyes. She wears more jewelry than my mom—fake pearls, decorative broaches, large clip-on earrings. I especially like her butterfly pins. Butterflies and the color yellow are Grandma's favorite things.

My mom talks to her for a little while in the kitchen, and I decide to explore the house. The family room is brown—brown carpet, wood paneling, and brown couches. There is a painting on the wall of a beautiful woman with blonde hair and blue eyes. I'm not sure which of my aunts it is. Down the hall, there is a pink bathroom. The toilet seat is padded. The bathtub is rusty and old and scares me a little.

To the right of the bathroom is my Grandma's bedroom. It is also pink, but a warmer shade. The bed has a floral comforter, and is too tall for me to climb up on. Across from the bed there is a wall, and on the wall there is a crucifix—it is about a foot tall, made of dark, polished wood. It scares me, but I always stare at it anyway. I know who the man on the cross is—it's Jesus. I've seen this image before in my Children's Bible. But in that picture, Jesus' face just looked sad—in this one, he looks like he is hurting. There is blood leaking from his wrists where the nails are—whenever I notice this, I have to look away, because blood makes me feel sick.

My mom doesn't like the crucifix. She told me we won't ever have one in our house, and it is important to remember the good things that Jesus did, not the way he died. My mom doesn't like church either—she says that we worship God by spending time in nature. On Sundays, we go bike riding, skiing, or boating, depending on the season, because my dad isn't working and those are his favorite thing. Ski boots hurt my feet. The motor of the boat makes a terrible noise. I am bored of doing the same thing every week, so I bring toy animals and don't talk to anyone. Then my dad gets mad, and he and my mom talk about why they wish I was like Steve and Bernadette's kids, because those kids are *enthusiastic.*

I walk through the second door in Grandma's bedroom, which leads to a room with green walls. I call it The Indian Room because there is a ceramic Indian on the bed stand—it is actually a very old bank for coins. This is the room where my mom and some of her sisters slept.

The door in The Indian Room leads to the last room, which has blue walls. It is bigger than the others, and I don't know who used to sleep here. There is a bed next to a big bookshelf that is built into the wall. There are wooden chairs, painted blue, and also a blue closet. That is where Grandma keeps the fur coats.

The snow leopard coat is fine, because that one is fake fur—so is the lion coat. But the shawl is made out of minks, which are like wild ferrets. Luckily, Grandma didn't buy it—it belonged to someone else in our family, long ago. I love animals more than anything, and I hate hunters and I hate ladies like Cruela Deville who wear fur coats—but I also love to wear Grandma's fur coats and pretend I am a leopard, lion, or mink.

I lie on the bed for a while, in the blue room, looking at all of Grandma's books on the shelves. They are adult books, with many pages and no pictures except the covers. They are pictures of ladies in fancy dresses, looking up at men with big muscles and no shirts. I wonder what kinds of secrets these books must hide and wonder at all the things Grandma must know from reading them. There is a picture of Jesus' face pinned on the wall, so I figure that they must be books about God.

Mom and Grandma come into the blue room and find me. Mom sits in one of the chairs. I ask Grandma to play with me, and she does. We put on her fur coats—she is the lion and I am the leopard. The coat is way too big on me and drags on the floor. We prowl and growl and sway from side to side, moving all around the room. My imagination runs wild with stories. We continue to prowl until Grandma is tired and sits in a chair. Then I decide to play my other favorite game—the one where Grandma is an old lady and I am her cat. I crawl into her lap and she pets my head and I purr.

Grandma is the only person I will sit with. My mom and dad sometimes get me into their laps with the promise that they'll read me a story—but beyond that, I don't like being touched. I never tell anyone, but it is because most people don't *see me*. I don't feel like myself when they hold me, and I get sad. Grandma is the only adult who I know can see me right.

We head back to the kitchen. I have a cup of water to drink and sit at the table with Grandma and my mom. They sip their tea and Grandma eats a baked potato with real butter. On the wall, there is a drawing of a dog's face carved into the soft wood. My Grandpa accidentally drew it on there, my mom says. He's dead now. I don't know how someone accidentally draws on a wall, but I don't ask. There are also stain-glass pictures of multi-colored butterflies hanging on the windows, glowing in the sunlight.

Everyone is happy. We tell Grandma about our week, and she tells us about her week. Then it is time to leave. Grandma doesn't hug or kiss me this time either. She steps out on the porch and waves as we get into the car.

Watch out for dragons! she says.

She never said it before I was born, and no one is quite sure what she means. My aunt thinks she means to keep away from people that will hurt us. I don't think so, because I like dragons. People just misunderstand them, because they are scared of getting burned by their fire-breath. Grandma knows better, because she understands things like that. She just worries that I will get burned by accident if I don't watch out, so she has to warn me. That's her job.

Rolley Poley

After my baths, Dad and I wrestle. He throws me in the air and I land on the bed. I beg for him to do it again and again. He scratches his unshaved face against my stomach and says, Tummy meat! I squeal and laugh like a little pig. He puts me in a headlock and pretends to punch me in the gut. Then he takes me in his arms and we tumble back and forth.

Rolley…Poley!

We chant this together.

Rolley…Poley!

Rolley…Poley!

Rolley….Whitey!

We say this when we bump into Whitey. She's our white cat and she is trying to relax on the edge of the bed. Whitey is a female but Mom and Dad call her *he* and say he is more like a male. He/she howls all day and has stinky feet. Blackie is our other cat. She is all black. They don't get along, and sometimes they fight, which is sad but exciting.

One time when we are wrestling, Dad throws me on the bed like usual, but this time I bounce too hard and right off of the bed. I hit my head on the nightstand on my way to the floor and it makes me cry. After that, Mom invents gentle wrestling. It's just cuddling. Nobody likes cuddling, so pretty soon we go back to regular wrestling.

Dad reads me bedtime stories, and doesn't stop until I fall asleep. Sometimes he picks me up and raises me over his head, then brings me back down again. He says, Up to the ceiling and down to the floor! In the winter, he takes a rope and hooks up my sled to his bike. He pulls me around the neighborhood, and I always sing, Walkin' in a winter wonderland…Our favorite games is to count the cats we see.

At Christmas time, I ask again and again to see the baby Jesus. Dad takes me to Saint Rose Church where there is a life-size manger. It's amazing to see the baby Jesus and his family in person because we read about him in a Christmas book. Dad laughs because I think it's so great. It makes me happy that he is happy. Then one day, he stops being happy.

Dad works everyday at the hospital, except weekends. I used to go to the babysitter, but now Mom is staying home with me. She worked at Catholic Charities for the poor children in the city. Now that Mom doesn't work for the poor children, we can hang out all day. We go to the zoo, or the park, and we make arts and crafts. We play imagination games. When she's in the kitchen, I get on my hands and knees and I crawl towards the counter. I knock on the wood, pretending it's a door. Mom answers the invisible door. She is the little mermaid.

Who's there? She says.

It's me, I say.

Who are you?

I'm Pongo, I say.

What is a Pongo?

I'm a dog.

A dog fish?

No, just a dog!

We go on like this for a while. The other game is called Change.

I'm so happy today! Mom says. She sings and dances while she makes my lunch. *I've got sunshine on a cloudy day. When it's cold outside, I've got the month of May…*

Change! I shout.

She slows down everything she's doing. Oh I'm so sad today...

I laugh like a maniac. Change!

I'm happy again! Mom says. *Well I'd guess you'd say, what can make me feel this way?*

But then Dad comes home from work, and all the fun has to end. First we have to rush to clean up before he arrives. Dad yells at the kitchen table, telling Mom about the stupid people at the hospital. I don't really understand. While he yells, I'm not allowed to talk to Mom. I go and play with my dinosaur figurines and feel cranky.

Dad doesn't talk to me much anymore. Even at dinnertime, he just scowls. One time I try to tell a story about ancient Egypt and mummies, and he says, Can't we talk about the real world? He rolls his eyes and I feel embarrassed. Another time I ask him if he believes in ghosts.

What are you, stupid?

When Dad's nice again, I don't know if I can trust him. I hate weekends, because when he's around we don't have fun anymore. I can't be a dog or talk about anything that interests me. Mom isn't the little mermaid, and she doesn't sing. And there is always a set time that we have to be in the car and ready, and if we're not we get yelled at and called names.

One time I'm sitting on Mom's bed and watching her fold laundry. Why don't we leave Dad? I suggest.

She just laughs and continues folding laundry. I know it's always going to be this way.

One day when Mom is bringing in the groceries, Whitey runs out the door. No one sees it happen, but we can't find her/him afterwards. We put up signs and Dad goes searching every night on his bike. Eventually we give up. There is no more Rolley Poley Whitey, and no more howling or stinky feet.

A Pinch to Grow an Inch

When I'm six, I start school. I don't want to go, and I'm afraid to get on the bus. I cling to a stuffed dog and refuse to look at the other children. I just stare out the window. I wish I could stay home with mom, but I already waited an extra year and she wants to go back to work. The other kids are four and five, but I feel like the smallest one.

I don't like kindergarten. Never before have I experienced such injustice. Before I started, I didn't know there were adults who don't love children. Of course the teacher loves me, but that just makes it worse. She is terrifying.

There is one boy named Billy who sometimes acts out, but it isn't too bad. I like him enough. He just has trouble remembering to raise his hand. But he hates being called William. For whatever reason, it makes him lose it, and the teacher knows this. She provokes him, smirks, and then punishes him. One day, when we are getting our winter coats off the rack, the teacher has Billy's for some reason.

William, she says, Say please like we learned today and I'll give you the coat back.

I'm not William, I'm Billy! Billy says.

William, if you don't calm down and say please, you will miss the bus and you'll have to sleep at the school all alone.

He clenches his fists and eventually he is crying and screaming and pleading with her to please, just call him Billy.

Please, please, I want to go home!

I am very disturbed. Another time we have to color in pictures of bears with crayons. I make mine into a panda, and a girl named Rosa thinks it's funny. She decides to make her bear purple and pink. She stays in

17

the lines and everything, but the teacher won't hang it up with the others. She throws it out.

Bears are not purple and pink, she says.

Hasn't she ever heard of imagination? I despise her. And yet she adores me. It's sickening. When I get the chicken pox, she calls my mother everyday to ask how I'm feeling. It gets to a point where even my mother finds it strange and stops picking up the phone.

I don't like the way she favors me over the other students, but I especially don't like that she is touchy. I hate being touched. Mom always says that once I learned to walk, I never cuddled again. It makes Mom sad. I don't know why, but adults make me feel trapped. If they have books, they can trick me into sitting on their laps. But otherwise I am wild animal.

But this teacher is always hugging me. I am so scared that I start falling off my chair during class. We'll be in the middle of learning how to spell C-A-T, and slowly at first, I begin to slide sideways, until I drop hard onto the floor. Mom takes me to see a specialist about it.

The worst is on my birthday. Well it isn't actually my birthday—that's in August. But we celebrate the summer birthdays in June so it's fair for the summer babies. Two months before I am seven, we have cupcakes and punch. I hate both these things and don't eat. I also hate pizza and popsicles and cake and pretty much everything other kids like.

The teacher interrupts the other children's fun by making me come up to front of the room. Everyone is forced to watch as I am forced to lie, face down, across her enormous rippling thighs. I receive seven birthday spankings and a pinch to grow an inch. I think she does this on everyone's birthday. I can't remember. Regardless, it is horrifying.

Still, it is better being in the other kindergarten class. The kids discuss it on the playground in nervous, giggling whispers. The other kindergarten teacher's name is Mrs. *Sex*-ton. As in *S-E-X!*

A Seal Who Lives in the Ocean

In first grade, there is a boy in my class named Bradley. He has to wear prescription sunglasses all the time because of some eye problem. I also have to wear glasses and I'm self-conscious about them because most kids don't wear them at this age. They are big and plastic and make me look ugly.

Like most people, Bradley loves Power Rangers, and he always pretends he is the Pink Power Ranger, AKA Kimberly. He dresses up as her for the classroom Halloween party. But then one day, when there isn't even a costume party, he comes in dressed as a girl. He wears all pink and a blonde wig and says his new name is Kimberly. Everyone laughs at him and calls him a freak. The teacher probably told his mom, because he is dressed as a boy from that day on. It's kind of funny, because I wear boy's clothes but nobody cares.

Bradley and I play together sometimes at recess. It works well because I want to be the Red Power Ranger, Jason, and he lets me. Bradley and I aren't close friends, but I definitely play with him more than the other kids do.

One day we are sitting at our desks, and they are all pushed together to make groups, or "tables" as we call them. I am seated with Bradley and a girl named Kelsey, who is bratty. There are other kids around too.

Kelsey decides to pick on me. You have glasses, she says. You and Bradley *both* have glasses, so that means you have to *marry* him. She says this with such disgust, right in front of Bradley, as if marrying him is the grossest thing possible. Other kids laugh too, and I know that it isn't really about our glasses.

Kelsey ends up getting it in the end. Soon after, she takes a trip with her family to Bermuda, and comes back with a deep tan and beads in her fair. For show and tell, she brings in a large seashell. But when a boy named DeShaun goes to touch it, she shouts, No he can't touch it because he's black! Everyone gasps, and the teacher takes her out in the hall to have a long talk. I feel bad for DeShaun because he's the only black kid in our class.

Mom says Kelsey probably won't get in trouble, because she must have learned that somewhere, meaning her parents probably don't like black people either. So I guess that means it isn't her fault because she doesn't know any better. But I think she does know better, because we just learned about Black History Month, and it's her fault if she didn't pay attention.

One day I notice a girl named Sarah is drawing swastikas on her papers. I know what those are, because my cousins and aunt are Jewish and I know all about Nazis. Sarah even looks like a Nazi, because she has blonde hair and blue eyes. I ask her why she is drawing them and doesn't she know they are Nazi signs? She says no they aren't, they are her dad's sign because he has them all over clothes and flags and stuff that he collects.

I tell Mom and her eyes get really wide. She says sometimes she wishes she had stayed in the city and raised me there. I'm not sure what she means, but I think it is because she knew more black and Jewish people there, and less Nazis, and also Grandma.

On career day, a police officer comes into the classroom. He shows us his badge and his gun and tells us about arresting people, which I don't really care about. We are supposed to learn that the police are our friends, but the police aren't my friends, because they pull Mom over on the highway and yell at her and make her cry.

Then we have to get in a circle and the police officer asks what each of us wants to be when we grow up. Most the boys want to be police officers or firemen, and the girls want to be marine biologists. Bradley wants to be a nurse, and the police officer says, Why not a doctor? And Bradley says OK but he looks annoyed.

When it's my turn I say that I want to be a seal.

A NAVY Seal?

No, I say, I don't know what that is. I want to be a seal who lives in the ocean.

The police officer laughs at me and says that being a seal who lives in the ocean isn't a career. Everyone laughs at me. I decide that I want nothing to do with police officers or careers or laughing children. People always say I can be whatever I want when I grow up, but if I can't be a seal then what's the point?

Death and Kittens

Blackie dies in the springtime. It's even sadder than when Whitey ran away, because I can't tell myself that she found a new family who loves her. I'm sitting on the stairs when Mom tells me the news. They had to put her to sleep. I can't stop crying, and I just ask why over and over.

I was supposed to go to Nicole Vaughn's birthday party that day, but Mom calls for me so they know I can't come. She takes me to the garden store and we pick out a stone marker to be Blackie's gravestone. I'm still crying a little. Mom also let's me get some candy and something called a Chia Pet. It is a statue of a cat, and the back of the box shows how if you plant the seeds inside and water it, it will grow grass for fur. It's cool, but not as cool as Blackie.

When we get home, Dad has a cardboard box with Blackie inside. I look inside the box and there she is, lying on her side. I touch her black fur, but she doesn't feel right anymore. I say goodbye. Dad buries her behind the house in the woods by the creek.

Mom lets me stay home from school the next day. She gives me two statues from the dollar store to paint. They are cats with wings—angel cats. I paint one black and the other white. I feel a lot better knowing that Blackie and Whitey are in heaven and I will see them again someday.

A few days later, Mom gets a phone call from a nurse. Grandma fell when she was getting into bed, and she broke her hip. I start to cry and ask Mom if Grandma is going to die too. Mom says no, that she just has to go into the hospital and she'll be fine. We are going to visit her on Wednesday.

The next night, Tuesday, Dad and I are watching *America's Funniest Home Videos* on TV. There are videos of cats, dogs, babies—you name it—doing funny things on accident, caught on film. It makes us laugh. Mom is in the kitchen, washing dishes. The phone rings and she answers it. I can tell by her voice that something weird is going on. Then she starts to cry.

My insides are twisting and hurting with worry. She's in the other room now so that we can't hear her. Dad gets up to go ask her what's the matter. I stare at the TV, scared. My skin is made of needles.

When Mom tells me Grandma died, I don't cry at first. Apparently there was a clot in her blood that nobody knew about. I just stare at the TV screen. A man is being attacked by squirrels. I think to myself, Nothing in life is funny—I will never laugh again.

*

I have a framed picture of Grandma in my bedroom. I look at it when I'm sad, which is often. It is a full-length shot of her body. She is standing in front of a pine tree. On her right is the plastic statue of a baby deer that she had in her yard. She reminds me of Saint Francis of a Sissy, who I have on a card. Grandma gave the card to me because he is the saint of the animals. I put the card next to the picture in the frame.

One night, I dream we are together again. She is wearing the same royal blue skirt and blazer as in the picture. Saint Francis is there too, and he actually is sort of a sissy, because when he says hello his voice sounds funny, the way Bradley's does. The three of us walk together through a forest of deep green pines and other trees that shade us from the sun. It is either dawn or dusk—I can't tell. We are happy, but then I realize I am dreaming and that Grandma is dead. I start to cry, but she tells me don't be sad. You can always visit me in dreams, she says, and when you need me, just talk to me through the photograph, and if I don't respond, tell Saint Francis and he will find me.

When I am awake, I talk to the photograph often. I start to feel better.

Then comes the best day of my life. Dad picks me up from school because he is home from work early. He never comes home early, so I wonder what is happening. He says that there is a surprise for me at home. We park the car in the driveway and go inside. Mom is there and she leads us upstairs to my bedroom. Nothing is different.

Look under the bed, Mom says.

I get down on my hands and knees and peer under my bed. Curled up together in the far right corner are two little kittens.

They are brothers. One is a brown tabby, which I've wanted for as long as I remember. I name him Brownie. The other is white with tabby patches. Mom names him Spot.

It's hard to force myself to go to school. I want it to be summer vacation, so that I can spend as much time with the kittens as possible. During playtime, I write stories about Spot and Brownie 's adventures, complete with illustrations. When I get home, I staple the pages together to create books. I create other tales too—stories about Grandma, legends of how the animals got their names, informative essays on stegosauruses, and a chapter book series about an octopus who uses public transportation.

Don't Touch the Woodchips

Second grade starts out well. For the first time, I pick out my own outfits for school. Most days I decide to wear all denim: Lee jeans, a backwards denim hat and a denim jacket. I buy a patch of a deer at the bait store and ask Mom to iron it on my jacket. She says that it is for hunters. I hate hunters but I love deer, so I don't really care and I want it on there anyway. I pick out new brown glasses instead of the baby-pink-girly ones. Pink, baby, and girly are the worst words, in my 8-year old opinion. I wear animals tee shirts with environmentalist slogans such as "They Were Here First!" tucked in, with a braided leather belt and black converse high-tops. My thick brown hair is pulled back in a low ponytail, always. I hate that ponytail. I always carry a bizarre stuffed animal on my person. My favorite is a duck-billed platypus I got at the zoo gift shop. These are my favorite animals, after wolves and manatees. Oh and cats.

Needless to say, no girls in my class dress like me. Neither do the boys. But the boys appreciate my sense of style and I'm allowed to join their ranks. Dan, our leader, teaches us the rules of being a boy right from the start. We must hate *Titanic,* the Miami Dolphins, actual dolphins, Winnie the Pooh, and most importantly, all girls. Some kid mentions *I* am a girl. Dan is furious and says, No she's not! She's *different.*

I am so happy. I can hardly wait to tell my mother. I actually don't hate the girls. I'm just indifferent to them.

In the winter, we have to play inside at recess. The boys make their Beanie Babies battle or take risks by bungee jumping off desks or street racing in Tonka trucks. This results in several severe beanie baby injuries. Luckily, all the girls in my class are pretend veterinarians.

One day, misfortune strikes and my baby wolf catches the plague. I take him straight to the beanie baby hospital. The nurse who greets me is a girl named Jaclyn. She has short blond hair, glasses, and a stupid face for her age. It just doesn't work for her.

This wolf is sick, I say, placing him on a desk.

Some other girls come over to look.

You can't play, Jaclyn says.

I hate when people interrupt the most important moments by telling me I am playing.

That's not a real Beanie Baby, she says.

The other girls laugh at me.

I insist my wolf *is* a Beanie Baby, but Jaclyn shows me the tag. Sure enough, it says Bean Sprout. My wolf is a cheap, knock-off brand. I am ashamed that I don't live in Wildcreek. Kids in Wildcreek have *every* Beanie Baby.

Wildcreek is the most expensive housing development and the kids who live there make sure everyone else knows it. They flatter one another, describing to us how huge their friend's house is, and the friend will say, No, no, YOUR house is the hugest! If you live anywhere else, you're basically a scrub.

I imagine their housing development to be a magic land of swimming pools and backyard-playgrounds and dozens of friends on the same street who have sleepovers every night. What's worse is I'm pretty sure I am right.

Another staple of second grade life is Don't Touch the Woodchips. This game is essentially tag, but with more injuries. It is played by chasing one another, at full speed, on the metal jungle gyms. If you are tagged or your feet touch the woodchips AKA. lava, you are out. Naturally, it is boys vs. girls. Whoever has the most survivors at the end is the superior sex. The boys almost always win.

I am still dressed all in denim and I'm still a boy at recess. I now hate the girls, and they know it. They hate me too, even more than they hate the regular boys. They have a symbol—they pretend it is top secret, but everyone knows it is the symbol for hating me. They draw it in the corners of their papers. It looks like an atom, like we learned about in science.

It is just another day, just another round of Don't Touch the Woodchips. I am chasing a girl named Caitlyn across the wooden bridge, and just as I am reaching out to tag her, she turns around and screeches in my face.

You can't tag me! You can't tag *anyone*, because you aren't a boy *or* a girl!

No one argues with her. Not even Dan. Several girls pipe in.

She can't play because she's not a boy or a girl!

The boys sort of shrug and go back to playing.

All the girls start chanting, You aren't a boy-oy, you're aren't a boy-oy!

I walk away to sit alone on the swings. I try to think about Brownie and Spot so I don't cry, but it's useless.

Manly Women

When I am ten, I discover manly women. I occasionally see a pair of them at the grocery store, and I hurry the other way. They are old and both of them dress like men. They have short, cropped hair, and look strangely similar. Whenever I see them, my stomach turns with anxiety. I try to silence the mean voices in my head. I don't like what they are telling me.

I don't understand how being gay works. I know what it means, because my dad explained it me when Ellen DeGeneres came out. It is when two girls or two boys are in love. Before that, I hadn't known that was allowed. I thought if you fell in love with someone who was your same gender, you would just be out of luck. I thought it would make for an amazing book or movie and I figured I was the first person to come up with the idea.

What I don't understand is the logic behind gay relationships. If you are a gay man, that means you act like a woman. So why are gay men attracted to each other then, since they aren't attracted to women? The same with lesbians—if they are more like men, then why do they want to be together? It seems like an inherent flaw in the design.

I try to focus on make-believe, in and out of school. I don't need other children either. I am constantly someone or something else in my mind, and soon it is second nature. If I see a movie I like, I warp into the hero almost immediately after leaving the cinema. The characters are my true identity—the girl who lives day to day, owns dolls, plays soccer, and practices the violin is not. I'm really Aladdin, or Simba, or Han Solo, or Peter Pan, depending on the day.

Before third grade begins, my second grade teacher calls in my mom for a meeting. She is concerned about my development because I am a tomboy. She thinks it is best to split me up from Dan and the other guys so that I can try to socialize with girls. Otherwise, I will grow up to be a manly woman. Or worse, Ellen Degeneres.

Gay and Proud

My third grade teacher is stern, but I like her OK. I'm nervous around the students though, because I hardly know any of them. One day we are standing in the hall, split into in boy and girl lines as always. A girl name Karen is looking at me.

Why do you have holes in your jeans? she says. It's less a question and more of an accusation. Everyone else has nicer clothes, I notice. The girls all dress the same, and it is important that you have butterfly shaped hairclips and that you buy your outfits from Limited Too, The Gap, or Old Navy. I've never heard of any of those except The Gap. I have a white tee shirt that says Gap on it, so I wear it to school. One of the cool boys says it stands for Gay And Proud and they all laugh, so I don't wear that shirt again.

I get new jeans, but Karen has a problem with those too, because they aren't bellbottoms. She calls them high-waters, which means they are too short to wear, unless there is a flood and you don't want your pants to get wet. When I tell my mom, she remembers people saying that when she was little and she knows that it's one of the worst insults ever. We go shopping right away.

I get a pair of bellbottom jeans and some new shirts that have shorter girly sleeves. I feel a little awkward, but I made sure nothing I bought was too girly, but only girly enough so that no one thinks I'm weird. What I really want to buy are the wicked cool boy pants that have zippers on them and *transform into shorts*. Mom buys me a pair, but I only wear those when no one is around and I don't have school. Same with my caps and old tee shirts with the animals on them. I even buy some butterfly clips for my hair, and fruity flavored lip-gloss. It tastes good. When no one is looking, I lick it.

At first I feel cool, but then I start to worry because everyone at school uses gel pens with colorful ink, and I just have regular pens and pencils. Luckily Mom buys me some gel pens. But then one day, Karen laughs and says, Why do you wear the same pants everyday? Are you a scrub?

Scrubs are poor, dirty, smelly people who live in Mattydale and listen to Hanson instead of the Backstreet Boys. Some of them live near me too but I'm not like them because I like the Backstreet Boys and N'SYNC and the Spice Girls like you're supposed to. When someone asked me my favorite song at the beginning of the year, I didn't know anything and I felt so stupid. I always liked that song that goes *bye bye Miss American Pie* but I didn't know what it was called and I figured that was a stupid thing to like. I asked my mom what to do, and she said next just tell people my favorite song is "The National Anthem" because that should be *everyone's* favorite song.

I hate looking like a scrub. I don't think Mom will buy me another new pair of bellbottoms, and even if she did, Karen will find another problem to tease me about. She says my hair is too thick, and whenever I'm really happy about something like story time she says, Geez calm down, so I feel really embarrassed about myself.

One day I find Mom in the kitchen like usual.
Mom, would you be mad if I grew up to be gay?
Mom looks thoughtful for a moment.
Not mad, she says, Just very sad.
She explained how people like that live on the fringes of society, and how it is hard enough to find

love when you are normal. It's a horrible life, she says, I don't want that for you.

Thank God I have a crush on a boy. His name is Timothy O'Connor. He wears awesome striped shirts, has a cool blonde mushroom haircut, has lots of freckles, and plays soccer just like me. I realize I love him when he stops Robert Giocondo from killing a spider and captures it in a cup to set free outside. That is the same thing I do for bugs and spiders, and I think he is just about the best person I've ever met.

Unfortunately he is also really cute so all the girls like him and take his attention. I just love him from afar. I know that I'm weird and not like the girls. Something is wrong with me, and someone like Tim will never like me back.

Roxboro Road Middle School of Witchcraft and Wizardry

Starting in fifth grade, I'm at a new school called Roxboro Road Middle School. There are tons of new kids from elementary schools all over the district. Karen still bullies me. It's the third year she's been in my class. In fourth grade, she and the popular girls also ganged up on a girl named Alessandra and decided not to be her friend anymore. I always liked Alessandra, and we became friends. It my mind, it was perfect—it was us against the world.

Alessandra is Italian, with olive skin, black hair and light blue eyes. She's very pretty. Her family has the biggest house in Wildcreek, with a pool and a jungle gym in the backyard. She also has a crush on Timothy O'Connor, and I think he might even like her back. My feelings for him haven't changed, but I'm not that jealous because I like to spend time with both of them together.

But in fifth grade, Karen decides she wants to be Alessandra's best friend again. Even after how mean Karen was, Alessandra ditches me for her. Every time we have to break into partners, I hope that Alessandra will pick me, but she never does. It's very confusing, because she still calls me every night to talk, and she invites me over to go swimming on weekends.

One day in early September we are hanging out at her house and we go upstairs to her bedroom. She takes off her swimsuit right in front of me and I'm paralyzed with shock. She asks me if she is fat. I'm embarrassed and can't look, but I say no, because she isn't. Then she tells me that she wants to practice kissing on me, so that she can kiss boys right. I don't know what to do. She sits on my lap. I'm still in my swimsuit. We sit in silence.

It's like your Santa Claus, she finally says.

I don't say anything.

Ask me what I want for Christmas.

Uh, what do you want for Christmas?

Little girl, she adds with an encouraging nod.

What do you want for Christmas, *little girl*?

I want you, Santa Claus! She makes a kissy face then explodes with laughter. To my relief, she stands up and gets dressed without really kissing me.

She repeats the Santa routine pretty regularly for kicks, except clothed, thankfully. But school, it's like I don't even exist. Karen won't let me or Tiara Jones sit at the fifth grade girl's lunch table, probably because Tiara is black and I am weird. This seat is taken, Karen will say if we try to sit down. So the two of us sit at a table alone. I try to talk to Tiara, but she moved here from a different district, she's girlier than me, and we don't have much in common.

Benny Novak sees us and says we should sit with him. At his table, there are a few other boys—most the boys sit at the fifth grade boy's table, which is next to the fifth grade girl's table. Those boys don't really talk to us, and just trade Pokemon cards.

Benny is really small—like less than five feet tall. He has as blonde mushroom haircut, but it doesn't look cool like Timothy O'Connor's. He has braces, and wears his shirts buttoned up all the way. He's very hyperactive and talkative. He asks me lots of questions. I find him pretty annoying, but he ends up being my only friend. At least I have a partner now.

People start saying Benny and I are going out, and they laugh at us. He doesn't seem to mind, but I do. Then everyone starts saying that they think Benny is gay. I start wondering if it's true—I'd rather he were, because I don't want him to have a crush on me.

He gives me a copy of his Harry Potter book and tells me I should read it. He's obsessed with Harry Potter, and I don't see what all the fuss is about. Then I start reading it, and I can't stop until I've read all three.

From that day forward, I am Harry Potter.

Of course I don't tell anybody, because I'm a big kid now and we aren't supposed to play make believe. Plus, I bet it would be obvious that it's more than make-believe for me. Because I never stop—I'm secretly Harry Potter every day. I am a first year student at Hogwarts School of Witchcraft and Wizardry, and I'm a pretty big deal there.

One day, Karen is teasing Benny because he has acne. I tell him Karen is a Slytheryn—one of the evil wizards. He thinks that's really funny, and we start trying to figure out who everyone would be if we lived in Harry Potter's world. He says he'd be Harry Potter. I say that's stupid, because I'm the one who has black hair, green eyes, and glasses. Plus, we both know I'm braver and better at sports, and my personality is more like Harry's. He would be Neville Longbottom.

He says none of that matters, and that I have to be Hermione because I'm a girl.

But I'm nothing like Hermione, I say. You be Hermione.

He keeps saying he's the boy and that makes him Harry Potter automatically, and I'm a girl so I'm Hermione.

I can't argue with that. I hate him and I stop talking to him for a few weeks. Then one morning in music class, I notice that his ear looks funny. I get a closer look. It's all red, and blood is trickling out of it.

I ask him what happened and his face gets really red. Nothing, he says. I keep pushing him to tell me, and he mumbles something about his step dad but how it's no big deal.

I tell the teacher about it. She thanks me and says she will take care of it. Mom says I did the right thing. I hope so. At least Benny doesn't come to school bleeding anymore.

Cafeteria Catholics

I can't sleep at night. I find myself wondering what dead bodies look like. I can't seem to keep the images out of my head. It's so horrible, but the more I fight it, the more persistent the images and the dreams.

I wake up Mom one night. What if there is no God?

Don't worry, she says, There is.

But what if there's not?

The idea of not existing anymore terrifies me. It's not that I love life, I'm just sickened by the pointlessness of it all. I would no longer be conscious. I would have no thoughts. I would no longer be, period. How could things be, without me?

I will die, I remind myself over and over at night, tossing and turning in bed. I will die. Mom will die, Dad will die. Everyone will die and rot.

Alessandra tells me on the phone that my problem is I don't have faith because I don't go to church. She and her family are Catholic they believes in Jesus. She also believes in Santa and the Easter bunny, like all Catholics.

I haven't believed in Santa or the Easter bunny or Jesus since I was three or so. But I try really hard. I see a rabbit on my way to the bus stop, and I try to get excited. I start wearing a gold cross necklace that I got when I was born.

Every night, I read from *The Children's Bible* Grandma gave me long ago. It is illustrated with cartoons. I can't comprehend the stories. It's not that they don't make sense. It's just I'm not quite sure what they are supposed to tell me, beyond the obvious. Maybe if I read the real Bible? I try, but I don't get past the first few paragraphs…it's really boring. Maybe I'm over thinking it.

Mom is impressed that I read the whole *Children's Bible*, and that I read all three Harry Potter books. She gets me other books, and I read them too. I read all the time. I used to find it difficult, but now I can't stop. I read about dinosaurs, ancient Egypt, time-travelling cats, and all the Wayside School books.

I ask Mom which religion we are. She says nature is our religion, and that is why we go for bike rides and walks on the parkway. I look at her doubtfully. She shrugs. If anyone asks say you are Catholic, she whispers. It turns out I am, because she baptized me herself. Just in case, she says. But don't tell Dad.

Why don't we go to church? I ask.

She says we just never have the time. She looks uncomfortable.

Is Dad Catholic?

She says no, he's a Presbyterian—or he used to be, but his family stopped going to church because Uncle Bob dropped the money jar and said, God dammit! in front of the whole church. Sometimes she wishes we did go to church because then I would have a community. Maybe she made the wrong decision, she says. I feel guilty for bringing it up.

She tells me when she was little she wanted to be a nun. She begged to go to Catholic school, but Grandpa said no because he had bad experiences there and didn't want her to lose her respect for the priests and nuns. She had to go to public school like everybody else, but at least the Catholic kids got to leave early to go with the nuns to learn about Jesus. She laughs as she recalls how they had a whole lesson devoted to what to do if you fall in love with a Protestant. It was a big deal. But it was OK in her case, because Grandpa loved Dad.

Grandma was Catholic too. She went to church all the time. Same with all Mom's sisters and my cousins on that side. Even though they all live far away, I feel more at ease around them than with Dad's family. The Connellys are in touch with the past and with the mysteries of the universe and our cousins in Ireland.

My dad doesn't seem to like the Connellys. He gets even crankier when they are around. He thinks the obsession with Ireland is goofy especially because the IRA are terrorists and no better than the people who tried to blow up the World Trade Center when Clinton was in office. Everything bad that ever happened is due to the Catholic Church, he tells me. Everything. The pope is probably a sociopath.

I ask him if he is Irish. He says no, he is an American and so am I. But he's wrong, because I'm Irish like my mom and the Connellys. That's why I have green eyes and freckles and I like to write. Irish people have the writer gene, according to what Grandma once said.

I decide I want to be Catholic. I ask Mom if we can go to mass. She's really happy. We get dressed up and go on Easter. I wear a white knitted hat and even a flowery skirt for her sake. We drive to Saint Rose, on Main Street.

We sit in the back. When the priest comes in, everybody sings a song, except me and Mom.

In the name of the Father, and of the Son, and of the Holy Spirit, the priest says.

Amen, everyone including Mom says.

Amen, I whisper.

The Lord be with you, the priest says.

And also with you, everyone says.

And also with you, I whisper.

We go to mass for a while on Sundays. Since none of the kids from school are there, I decide it is safe to dress like a boy. Mom doesn't care, but people give me funny looks. Then we find out that people called mom a Cafeteria Catholic. This means that she picks and chooses Catholic rules to follow, like she is at the cafeteria buying her school lunch. That is apparently a bad thing, so we stop going to mass after that.

Amy Wagner

I walk into the classroom on the first day of sixth grade almost as nervous as I was in kindergarten. Neither Alessandra nor Karen nor anybody else is in my class, and I hardly know anyone in the room. I recognize a girl named April—she is blond, blue eyed, and mature-looking because she already has breasts. Her hair is always tied back, much like mine. Should I sit next to her? No, I would probably keep looking at her breasts, so it would be less awkward to sit with a stranger. I wonder what homeroom Benny is in. Hanging out with him would be better than nothing. Then I see a girl slumping in the back row on the far right. I instantly am drawn to her.

Her name is Amy Wagner. She is rather plain looking. Her hair is shoulder length, brown, and lusterless, parted in the middle—small ringlets of bangs and dead ends frame her forehead. Her skin is milky, spotless, the hue of dough. Her eyes are pale blue, behind ovular metal glasses. Her nose isn't large, nor is it sharp, or a pig snout. It's a raindrop, if a nose can be such a thing. Her jeans are plain. Her sneakers are plain. She wears a white tee, depicting a rainbow flower. Up close, you can see that the flower is composed of elongated soccer balls.

I sit beside her and start talking, but she doesn't say much. I'm picking up on a negative vibe. I don't think she likes me, but I don't especially care. I've heard a bit about her. She was in one of my classes the previous year. She's smart, I know that much, because she's in the gifted program. I'm not, and I've got a chip on my shoulder about it—mostly because Mom has a chip on her shoulder about it. Benny once suggested that Amy would make a good Hermione for our Harry Potter fantasy—the responsible, doting, goody-two-shoes friend. I hadn't known Amy then, so I scoffed. But now I am keen to cast her in the role.

She definitely doesn't like me at all. She gives me haughty glances over her glasses as I talk. She's all but silent. Why am I so talkative? I feel cocky and I can't turn it off. This energy only comes from pretend and never during school hours. What's happening? I feel like myself, and that isn't allowed in public.

I'll win her over. I'm determined.

In reality, I already have. I tease her and she gets huffy. I literally wink at her once from across the room. And as the year goes on, I find that for the first time, I have a best friend who likes me back. There's another person on this planet besides my mother who is interested in what I really have to say.

*

It starts at April's sleepover.

I awake in confusion, grabbing at my hair. There's something crawling in it. Amy is kneeling beside my head. She quickly retracts her hand.

Why were you touching my hair? I ask.

I wasn't, she says.

I let it go and I fall back to sleep because I'm really tired. But its weird, and I feel really uncomfortable. Even days later, I can't seem to shake the feeling.

*

Ruth, my neighbor in fifth grade, knows Amy's family. She tells me a story on the bus.

Amy's mother didn't know she was pregnant at first. Her husband got mad and pushed her down the stairs, and then she had to go to the hospital. That's when she found out she was going to have Amy.

Her parents are divorced now, but Amy still has to visit her dad in Solvay on the weekends. Ruth tells me that he still threatens Amy's mother. He leaves dead fish on the windshield of her car, which is a symbol from the Mafia that means soon you will be sleeping with the fishes.

I don't tell Amy that I know this. One night on the phone, she starts to cry. She won't explain what's the matter. It seems like she's always crying, even in school. She barely talks or eats at lunchtime. Over the phone, she asks me if I can keep a secret. I say yes. She tells me that her dad hit her. She says the last time it happened was the summer.

Amy doesn't like birthday cake—I know this about her, because I don't like it either. Her grandma made her one for her birthday, but she didn't want to eat it. Her dad was drunk and angry, and he took her in a back room and beat her up for ten minutes. He told her she was ungrateful.

I don't know what to say, except that I'm sorry. She tells me she's so glad she met me. I'm the best thing that ever happened to her, she says. I still don't know what to say.

The next day I find a handmade card in my locker, made of yellow construction paper.

Thank you for being my best friend, it says, written in a rainbow of crayon colors. I find Amy by her locker, and I give her a hug. It's very uncharacteristic of me, but I've never cared this much about anyone. I want to hold her like this forever, or at least until she feels better.

*

Can I play a song for you? Amy asks.

49

She's being weird on the phone, as she often is. Long stretches of silence, random bursts of tears—but I'm willing to put up with it. I'm like the wind, she tells me, and she's the ocean. I don't know what that means, but I think it's beautiful. When the wind blows now, I feel strong.

I've started dressing like a boy again. I wear my swishy wind-pants everyday with sports tee shirts. I pull my hair back, and sometimes I daydream about chopping off the ponytail. I have a best friend now, so I don't care what other people think. I'm actually pretty popular too, because I'm the best athlete and best artist in the class. Amy isn't good at sports or art, only spelling and math and stuff. Nobody really likes Amy, but everyone likes me, so she is protected.

She plays the song on a CD player and puts the phone by the speaker. I'm having trouble hearing it over the static. It starts slow and sad, making me roll my eyes. I'm sitting on the carpet in my bedroom, the phone pressed to my ear. I strain to pick out the lyrics.

I never had a dream come true
Til the day that I found you
Even though I pretend that I've moved on
You'll always be my baby
I never found the words to say
You're the one I think about each day
And I know no matter where love takes me to
A part of me will always be with you

I feel a surge of dread. I don't know exactly what's going on, but this sounds like a good-bye song. Is she moving away, I ask?

She tells me she isn't. Can she tell me something though?

Yes. My heart is pounding.

I'm gay, she says.

What? I start to cry, but I try to hold back the sound. No you can't be, I say. Never in my wildest dreams had I expected this.

I can't help it, she says, I just am.

You have to try not to be, I say. The panic is building. Oh god, if *she's* gay, than what am *I?*

I have to tell you something else, she says.

No, I say. I hang up.

She calls back.

I pick up because I can't help it. What?

I have to tell you something, she says, Please.

I don't want to know.

I think I'm in love with you, she says.

I hang up again, this time for good.

I run to the bathroom because I feel like I might be sick. I look at my reflection in the mirror. If Amy loves me, that must mean I'm gay too. Otherwise why would she be attracted to me? My eyes scan my body. Does she find me sexy? I feel sick again and start to cry. I don't want to be sexy!

Downstairs, Mom is watching a James Bond movie from the 1970's. James Bond kisses one of his Bond girls. I can't watch. Love is ruined, I think. Forever. Mom asks me what's wrong, and I tell her nothing. I need to go for a walk.

I head down the street towards the elementary school, filled with shame. I am corrupted. I am dirty. Everything I've done up until this point has been a lie. I'm going to have to run away. I don't know how, but I can't possibly stay here now. One day I'll write a book, I think, or a movie. *My best friend is gay,* it will begin, and *she is in love none other than... (dramatic music) Me!*

No, it's more like a sitcom, I think, growing bitter. I imagine other people laughing. *Hahaha! You two are lesbians! Which one's is the boy? Haha neither 'cause you're both girls!* No. I won't let this happen.

When I get home, I call Amy back. I tell her that I'm not gay and that she has to stop liking me, immediately. Pick one of the boys in our class and force yourself to like him, I tell her. Who is your favorite?

I dunno, she whispers. Paul is nice I guess.

Love Paul, I order.

She sniffles and says she'll try.

Next week, she is secretly dating a girl in the fifth grade instead and I only feel worse.

The Little Activist

Good morning *classth*, says Mr. Thompson, Today we're going to do *something thuper thpethal*. He says the s's with his tongue stuck between his teeth—a fake lisp. He uses a singsong voice, and he feigns a limp wrist gesture. It is clearly supposed to be an impersonation of gay man. I've seen it done on TV.

Several members of the class laugh appreciatively. I glance behind me at my two best friends, sitting at the other lab bench. Amy is staring absently at the forest mural in the front of the classroom. Benny is looking at his hands, his face the color of a strawberry.

OK you thilly goothes, Mr. Thompson says, Turn to page theven in your book!

He uses this stupid voice regularly. But today I've had enough. I raise my hand.

Yes thuper star? He calls me this because I have over 100% in his class—I'm a *super star* and arguably the teacher's pet. During study hall and lunch, I take the class pets, two tortoises, out of their tiny aquarium in the biology room and outside, where I watch them munch on dandelions. Mr. Thompson figures I do this for his attention, or for the extra credit it earns me, but I really only do it for Sandy and Digger, the tortoises. They are cooped up all day, trapped in the classroom. I feel their pain.

I hesitate a second before speaking. I wish you wouldn't do that, I finally say.

He looks at me, faking confusion. What are you talking about, thilly goose!

Laughter.

Your voice, I say, When you do the fake voice, I…

I don't have the words. He looks at me like I'm a dumb girl. His patronizing eyes seem to dare me.

The Little Activist, he says, causing titters throughout the room. He's dropped the lisp.

He started calling me the Little Activist a few weeks prior when we were working on a lab. Math and Science assignments often pose hypothetical, real-world problems for us to solve. We were doing a plant-life unit, and one question was about someone attending a Farming College. Mr. Thompson had mocked it. I blurted, What's wrong with being a farmer? From that point on, he started calling me the Little Activist and asking me about my cows.

Why don't you like it? he says, in the voice, Because its *gay*?

I'm amazed that he actually says the word—I didn't think you were allowed to in school. I feel a flutter of panic, wondering, Does he know? Would he make the same assumption as when I defended the farmers? Would he tell the class I must be gay, too?

I don't answer.

He smiles a simpering, sympathetic smile, as if to say, You don't have to be one of them. There's still time.

I won't smile back.

The Darien Lake Field Trip

I'm walking through the crowds, and I'm seeing everything differently. There are couples everywhere. A man hands a girl a rose, and she laughs and embraces him, tip-toed, arms around his neck. There is an ache in my chest and my eyes burn. The sun is bright. I am thirteen years old.

I want to undo the realization, but it is too late. It's impossible to willingly un-know something. The thoughts entered my mind uninvited, and they wish to tumble from my lips with equal incivility. The urge to confess is overwhelming.

Benny is beside me. He walks on his toes, a slight bounce to his step. His blonde hair is straight, parted in an "M" at the widow's peak. He's taller now, but scrawny, and unbecomingly effeminate. His nose is big and his chin is small. His eyes betray a lack of intellect, and a pubescent disregard for complexity. He's looking around for another person he'd rather be with than me. He's always scanning for ways to climb the high school social ladder. I do love him, even though he can be annoying. He's become like a brother to me.

I have to tell you something, I say. My throat has constricted, making it hard to get the words out. I know tears will soon fall.

What's wrong? he asks, barely glancing my way.

Let's sit.

We find a park bench off to the side of the crowded path, facing a large carousel. We sit watch as the ride begins, momentarily enchanted. Small children and their parents straddle the painted ponies and begin their orbit. Some horses move up and down on the pole as well. I remember it being an event—a right of passage even—when I was brave enough to ride those ones. My mom and I would stop sometimes at the Carousel Mall. She would hand me the large, shiny gold token with an embossed pony on its face. But I can't think about my mom right now. It's too painful.

The night before, Amy and I talked on the phone as usual. Though we like to conceive of ourselves as extraordinary, we were excited, just like everybody else, for the end-of-the-year field trip to Darien Lake. Unfortunately, Amy had fallen in love with yet another girl—something that made my stomach turn for more reasons than one.

This girl's name is Li. She is small, thin, nerdy and awkward, but in an adult's eyes, perfect. Even if she is gay (which I doubt) she won't be able to face it—not at this age. And if on the off chance she is gay, and does face it, she still won't be interested in Hot Topic-wearing, white trash like Amy.

But Li is polite, and I know she'll put up with Amy's wooing, to a point. And it is just my luck that the point will probably occur *after* the trip to Darien Lake.

Amy had been going on about which roller coasters she intended to ride for a good half hour before I butted in.

Can we be partners though? School trips always employed the buddy system. When she responded in the negative, I said, Can I at least hang out with you guys? No clear indication was made either way.

And so I spent the day trailing after her as she trailed after Li and her friends. They seemed to tolerate Amy, because she was putting on an angelic little act. No one suspected her sinister motivations. Even at age thirteen, I knew Amy was hoping to catch Li alone, to make a move.

I stood by the wave pool—you know the kind, a big walk-in swimming pool at amusement parks that simulates the tides. I stood awkwardly in my little one-piece bathing suit with boy shorts over it and watched Li, Amy, and the other girls laugh and splash, all ignoring me. No boy shorts on them. I'd never felt so lonely.

I watched as Amy bought a giant lollipop—rainbow colors, swirled—the old-fashioned candy shop kind. She gave it to Li, and aw, isn't that sweet of her? I hated Li and tried to incinerate her with my gaze. Though really, I wouldn't have wanted the lollipop. I don't like candy, and I don't like being doted upon. I'm not the girl here.

My masculinity had been bruised almost beyond repair. Here was this girl—this Amy—so much more the feminine one, yet gutsier than I in every way. I could play sports, I could climb the gym ropes, and I had refused to wear a dress for years. Hadn't *I* been the rescuer? Hadn't *I* protected *her*? And yet Amy cut her hair short, while I stood there terrified with my ponytail. And now she was wooing other girls, and I was jealous of them! What did it all mean? What was I becoming?

What is it? Benny asks.

It's as though I can feel the earth's rotation. I've been thrown off my kilter. My self-perception is shot, and I'm being forced into a corner. This wasn't how I wanted it to happen. The fairground organ plays, eerily upbeat, mocking me.

I think, I say, I might like Amy.

The organ notes continue, and the fairy lights twinkle and bounce off the mirrors.

Are you gay?

No. I don't think so. I mean, I don't know what I am.

He sighs. Oh man. This is not good. I mean, you're still my BFF. But this isn't good, is it?

I don't answer. I'm watching the children on the horses, gripping the poles. Don't they know those are a hotbed of germs? The parents are equally naïve, standing beside in case their child should slip from the saddle. What is it about those classic carousels? Even at age thirteen, they make me feel so old. I'm looking back on my childhood, but it's not really my life at all. It's an imitation—an illusion of forward movement and free will—an unbreakable, inevitable circle. Everyone is grinning, but I don't know why. Many childhoods are miserable, and the happy ones end too soon.

The Red Notebook

That summer I find dark blood stains in my underwear. I know what it is, but somehow I hadn't known it was coming for me. My chest begins to change. It swells, like little balloons slowly filling with air. I start shaving my legs and armpits, because, well, that's what's expected.

North Syracuse Junior High, somewhat strangely, houses only eighth and ninth graders. It combines the two middle schools, and therefore half the student body is composed of complete strangers from Gillette Road Middle School. We consider them to be preps, except for Bridgeport kids—they consider us to be poor, except for Wildcreek kids. But soon everyone forgets and we all mix together in misery. New hierarchies are formed.

Nervous, bored, and in need of an outlet, I carry a red spiral notebook with me everywhere I go. In the notebook, I write poetry. Most of it is of romantic and erotic longing—much of it involves Amy. When I am bored in class, I write, and when I get home from school, I go up to my room and write some more. I close my eyes and wrap myself around a pillow, pressing to my stomach. It is pleasure and agony. I long without comprehension or release.

After school, Amy and I often hide up in the balcony of the empty auditorium. Sometimes we talk, usually about vague, philosophical things we only half-understand. Other times, we just sit in silence. Every time, the burning is there. Please let her touch me, I think. Please let her kiss me, lean on my shoulder, lie on the floor and pull me on down top of her. Anything.

She never does. But I can sense she feels the energy too.

One day, she steals my red notebook. We are staying after school with a purpose that day—we belong to *Synergy*, the school literary magazine. She knows I don't let anyone read my notebook, and so she takes it when I'm not looking. I beg her to give it back and I chase after her in the halls. It becomes a game of Monkey in the Middle as she passes it off to different kids, all of whom laugh and ignore my pleas. Eventually I give up and let Amy run off with the thing. I sit down, humiliated, leaning against the cool lockers, and I wait for her to return.

In a half hour or so, she walks down the hall towards where I sit. She hands the notebook back to me without saying a word. I follow her into the classroom. What's going on? No reply.

Amy gives me the silent treatment for the rest of November and I have no idea why. I am devastated. Please talk to me, I say, and she walks right on by. I wrack my brains trying to figure out what I did to deserve this. I apologize daily, without knowing why. I usually hide in the corner or in the bathroom during lunch period so that no one will see me cry. I hadn't realized until now how distanced I feel from all the people surrounding me. Without Amy, I am completely alone. What if she never talks to me again? I hang out at the park after school nearly everyday with Benny, speculating over my grim future as he half-listens.

December 1st it snows. I walk from the bus into school as it begins, enchanted with the swirling flakes. Inside, Amy is standing by my locker. And then, as if nothing happened, she begins talking to me again. Did you see the snow? It's beautiful...

She never gives any indication of what changed. I am relieved, but the damage is already done. I walk on eggshells from then on, careful not to upset her. I'm afraid that any wrong move could lead to abandonment. My depression is only held at bay by her fickle attention.

The Stupidest Thing I Ever Heard

By ninth grade, most of my friends have come out. Not publically, but to me at least. Benny is gay, Amy is a lesbian, and new friends like Gabriel (a theatre and band nerd from Cicero who was adopted from Korea as a baby), and Morgan (Amy's 13 year old, *Buffy the Vampire Slayer*-loving ex) are also embracing the label. In addition, I have many lesbian acquaintances through Amy. She hooks up with a lot of girls, and I try not to notice. I don't get along with any of them because all they talk about is sex.

I don't much care what my parents think anymore. They hate my new style, but whatever. I live for bands like Bad Religion, AFI, and The Dead Kennedys. I dress all in black and consider myself a punk. I cover my outerwear in safety pins and patches and wear flannels, thermals, and camouflaged army clothing. After Amy shows me some shocking photos of slaughterhouses, I become a vegetarian.

With Amy's approval, I even get the courage to cut my hair. I go at it myself, and it's a little jagged but not half bad. It reaches my chin, and I wear it in front of my face for the most part. That, coupled with the fact that I wear three sports bras under my clothes, enables me to pass as a boy. Still, I'm not a lesbian. I get angry at the very suggestion. On a few awkward occasions I settle on the label of bisexual, just to appease people. But I wouldn't touch any guys my age with a ten-foot pole. Not even Tim anymore. He's a jock and therefore, in my mind, the enemy.

Sometimes I go to the Gay Straight Alliance meetings. It's always a ruckus. The administration doesn't like the group—therefore, they refuse to fund it or pay a teacher to advise us. Umoja, the group for students of color, is in the same boat. The principal says they are purely social groups, and, impliedly, a waste of time. They tried to shut us down entirely but the district was afraid of a lawsuit. Due to lack of leadership, GSA meetings are addressed to either a packed, distracted room, or an empty, indifferent one.

What are you? a girl asks me the first time I attend.

I don't understand her question, or at least pretend as much.

Are you gay, straight, bi…?

I say I am nothing.

She says that means I am asexual.

I glare at her. I am not asexual.

The following week, she brings in a girly magazine with an article about teens that are something called transgender.

Maybe you're a boy trapped in a girl's body, she says.

I laugh. That is the stupidest thing I ever heard. You can't be trapped in the wrong body. Where is your right body?

One time in lunch, Gabe says, It's too bad girls can't get sex changes. You'd be a great candidate.

Yeah too bad, I say, smiling. I'd probably go for that. I mean, I'm not trapped in the wrong body—that's crazy talk. But if I could become a boy, I would. Then I wouldn't feel so mixed up all the time.

Sometimes I think that I'll find a way to fake having breast cancer so I can have a mastectomy. I daydream about dressing in drag and starting a new life in a new town. I'm an English teacher, and the kids all call me Mr. Dorsey. I wear fancy suits. I marry Amy and we get a house in the suburbs, next door to all our other friends and we live happily ever after.

Are You a Boy or a Girl?

One day, Amy and I stay later than usual after school and have to take a different bus home. This one stops at Roxboro Road Middle School first. It means we have to part ways and join the younger kids for the rest of the short ride home. Amy is headed to Mattydale and I to North Syracuse. But I stand with her by her bus, not wanting the moment to end. I say something that makes her laugh and she touches my shoulder with a dainty flick-of-the-wrist gesture, flirtatious but coy. Her hand rests for a millisecond before dropping again to her side.

Hey! a man's voice shouts.

We turn and see the red face of Mr. White, a history teacher neither of us had in middle school but that everyone knew. His presence is very flamboyant. He is a flabby and fat man in his thirties, with graying hair and a pointed nose. He seems perpetually sunburnt and sweating.

Why are you here? he yells at us. You aren't welcome here! This is a CHILDREN'S school

Calm down, I say, We're just standing.

I try to give him some credit. Maybe he's mad because we're older. But there are other older kids around too—that's how it works, day after day, if you stay after school. No. It is because, as far as he's concerned, we are two girls in punk clothes with short hair.

Don't move, Mr. White says, and he turns haughtily, like a cop with mission, and walks away from us.

Amy just sighs. I'll call you later.

OK, I say.

She waves, rolling her eyes, and gets on her bus headed to Mattydale. I ache to go with her, but know my mom would ground me. I also wasn't invited. She will probably have sex with her new girlfriend of the week, Sam, before calling me. When she does call, she'll probably say, Maybe I should break up with Sam...I don't know, And different variations of this for hours.

I get on my bus, which is mostly full of middle school kids. They are all staring at me. A small black girl with many braids says, Did you get in trouble? Did you *kiss* that girl?

No, I say, and I find a seat all the way in the back where I hope no one will bother me. I can tell I'm still being discussed, and I know why. The question will undoubtedly come, as it almost always does around children. I wait for it.

Are you a boy or girl? one boy finally asks, his friends giggling, clearly having dared him to speak.

What do you think? I ask.

"I think you're a boy. But you *might* be a girl who dresses like a boy."

"I'm whatever you want me to be," I say, putting on my headphones, proud that I have evaded the questions. It's one of those moments when the dialogue feels like a movie; when life works exactly how I would have written it. It is similar to the time some girl in the bathroom said loudly to her friend, so that I would hear, "If I were a dyke I'd just kill myself." I came out of the stall, put on the saddest face possible, and showed her the scars of shallow cuts on my wrists. "I'm trying," I said, holding my laughter in as the girl looked at me, too horrified to apologize...

I look out the window, listening to my music and watching as more children leave the building and head for their respective buses. Tiny kids with huge backpacks, and such babyish clothes. It's hard to believe Amy and I looked that young only a few years prior. It had been such a somber a time...how could anyone that small already be that serious?

I see Mr. White returning, still red faced, with the principal. They are looking every which way for Amy and me, but won't find us.

First Kiss

I don't need medication. This is one of many subjects on which my mother and I disagree. I feel that at age fifteen I should be the only one deciding what goes into my body. My mother and my shrink feel that forcing me to take Ritalin is in my best interest. I occasionally deceive her by throwing the pill in my mouth and hiding it under my tongue as I swallow my orange juice. I hold it there until I'm out the door, then spit it out and put it in the front pocket of my backpack. Over the course of the year I have acquired a formidable stash.

Amy takes them sometimes for performance enhancing purposes. If she has a math test for example, they will hype her up and help her focus. This morning, she doesn't want them though. She's still got my love life—or lack there of—on her mind. She started taking a bizarre interest the previous day when she commented on my virginity. Yes, I suppose I am a virgin. I had never really thought about it.

You need more experience, Amy tells me at her locker. She's lacing a tiny safety pin through the top layer of skin on her pointer finger. It would be alarming, but she always does that.

Why? I'm sort of exhausted by this talk.

Because no one will want to go out with you if you don't have experience. I know I wouldn't, she says giving me a meaningful look.

Great. I sigh. She's trying to convince me to date her ex, Morgan.

Speak of the devil, Morgan is coming down the hall towards us. Like me, she's more of a young boy than a girl. Her red hair is cropped even shorter than mine, so short it's almost a buzz cut. She's small, pale, freckly, and dresses in the requisite Hot Topic gear of our demographic.

Morning, she says.

Morning, I mumble.

Amy greets her with a look, as if to say, Go on.

Will you go out with me? Morgan asks me in a low voice. Her grey eyes are sunk deep in the sockets. She's avoiding my gaze, and her expression is unenthused. She's clearly only appeasing Amy.

OK, I say.

Morgan half-smiles. Cool, she says.

It's weird and we both know it. Two girls dating is one thing...but two people like us? We aren't supposed to mix. Why is Amy so insistent about it?

You two should kiss, Amy says.

Morgan moves towards me. I lean in, awkwardly placing my hand on her hip and bending down a bit. Are people looking? I don't want to do this. Not here, in the hall. It's my first kiss and I only get one.

Her lips are wet and feel plumper than mine. I don't like it. How do I know when to pull away?

Morgan pulls away first. She's blushing.

Dyke! A boy in a Jets jersey and sagging jeans is glaring and smirking at me. Carpet-munchers!

Several people have stopped to stare at me. Laughter.

See you at lunch, Morgan says. She does a good job of pretending not to notice, even when a crumpled paper ball hits her in the back of the head.

I feel dizzy. As Morgan and Amy walk away and the crowd abates, I realize I'll be expected to kiss Morgan again at lunch. And then at the buses. And every day after that...Christ.

I decide I'll write her a letter and give it to her before lunch. It'll explain that I'm breaking up with her for some fake, kindly vague reason. I'll have to hide in the art room until things blow over because I'm sure Amy will be furious with me.

I avoid Morgan and Amy for about a week. It's easy to skip lunch, because my meds have killed my appetite. I work on my drawings all period. My teacher, Mr. D, is really impressed with my commitment. Art is the only class in which I have an A. It's not that I'm stupid, I've just stopped doing homework. Which is actually pretty stupid. By the time I get home, I've crashed from the Ritalin and I just want to lie very still in the dark of my bedroom.

I wish Mr. D would come back into the room, because this guy is harassing me while I'm trying to work on my still-life.

You should make videos, he says, Of you and Amy doing stuff. I would pay you for it.

Leave me alone, I say.

Come on, he says, It'd be hot.

No! Go away.

Fuck you dyke, he says, You don't say no to me.

Fuck you I just did.

Luckily Mr. D is back. I'm a little afraid of this guy. He's started hanging out in the art room every day at this time, so there's no avoiding him. I'm going to have to go back to the lunchroom and face Amy.

Strangely, she forgives me right away.

I don't know, she says, Maybe it's kind of hot that you're a virgin.

Tyvek Homewrap

It's my first time visiting Amy's house. We go there straight from school. My mom seemed hesitant to allow me, but there was nothing she could say and she knew it. She's never liked Amy. She doesn't like how she treats me. Whatever, she doesn't understand.

Amy's house is small. The snow falls lightly around us as we walk up the driveway. In Mattydale, the neighborhoods are set up in a grid, a lot like New York City. Some are run down, and they all are older and smaller than the ones in my neighborhood. Amy is poor—I've known that for a while. Her house is under construction, covered in Tyvek Homewrap.

Tyvek Homewrap, I say quietly to myself.

Amy bursts out laughing.

What's so funny? I ask.

Tyvek Homewrap, she says.

I shrug.

We walk through the entranceway, kicking the snow off of our matching black converse sneakers. Amy has written song lyrics on the white rubber trim. I keep mine clean, because they were a gift and I know my mom would get angry if I ruined them.

No one is around but the cat, Jessie. He's big and orange, and runs away to hide when he sees us.

We sit on the wrap-around couch in the family room. The interior of the house is surprisingly fancy, with new furniture, plants, and a nice paint job.

Lets watch a movie, Amy says. She turns on the television. It's much larger than mine at home.

She puts in a DVD of *Edward Scissorhands*. I've seen it before, but I don't mind because it's one my favorites. Amy's too. We watch for a while in silence.

You know, Amy says, You kind of look like Edward Scissorhands.

I look at her, amused. What?

Yeah, especially if I mess up your hair a little more. She moves in closer and messes with it. I feel my blood get hot.

I'm gonna get some gel, she says, getting up.

She returns with a small container of a waxy, blue substance. She sticks her fingers in the goo then works it through my hair. It smells like coconuts. Her face is close enough that I could kiss her, if I dared. I look down instead, but that isn't much help. She's wearing a stretchy low cut white tank top and no bra. It's very clingy, and sheer. She's put on weight since the fall, and her breasts are a lot bigger. Most of her cleavage is exposed, especially when she leans forward. I swallow.

She notices me staring. I look away, but I'm blushing madly so it's no use.

Do you still like me? she asks.

I dunno, I mutter.

She reaches out and takes my hand in hers, lifting it through the space between us. She draws it towards her chest, placing it just above her left breast, on her bare skin. I exhale shakily as I begin to drag my fingers lower. She inches closer and I awkwardly drop my hand back in my lap. She's sitting so close now that are thighs are touching.

Yours is thinner, she says, putting her hand on my thigh.

Not much, I lie. I barely eat anymore, and have the BMI of Gandhi.

I'm fat, she says.

No you're not, I say. I can barely concentrated on what she's saying. Her hand is traveling up my leg. I don't breathe.

She begins to rub my inner thigh with her palm. Then she walks her fingers up to my button and fly, undoing them. She runs her fingers over the fabric of my blue underwear, lower, and lower, and I close my eyes, exhaling, melting into the cushions in ecstasy.

Whiskey Sleep Over

I stand in my briefs, looking in the bathroom mirror. With them on, I look alright from the waist down. I like my underwear. I've never really thought about it before, but I hope they are attractive. I'm going to lose my virginity tonight.

I can't stop thinking about Amy on the couch. I might die if it doesn't happen again soon. A week passed, and Amy hadn't so much as mentioned it. But today, Friday, at school, she asked me if I wanted to spend the night.

I wrap a towel around me and I go into my room. I pull on my boot-cut jeans and a slim gray tee with "Bright Eyes" written on it. Bright Eyes is a band—or rather, a guy in a band, Conor Oberst. I live and breathe his albums. Not a day passes when I don't listen to a Bright Eyes CD on my portable player. Amy introduced me to him, but I took a much more passionate interest. I've never related this much to anyone or anything—not even Amy, not even Harry Potter. It's like he is singing my thoughts out loud.

But this is the sound of the hopeless kids
as they scream from the basements of the
houses of their parents and
this is the sound of the hopeless ones
as they stare down at their books and
realize they have been lied to!

I sing as I pull on my socks and pack a change of clothes for tomorrow morning. I've been listening to a lot of new bands lately. Most people haven't heard of them except me and Amy, because they are indie, or old, or from England. I've decided that's what I want to do with my life—sing in a band. I've started recording myself singing as I strum an acoustic guitar. I use a portable karaoke machine I got for Christmas. Someday I want to transfer the cassette recordings to CDs, or maybe record them in a studio.

I can hardly contain my excitement as I take the stairs two by two. I wish my mom would hurry up and drive me to Mattydale. I'm losing my virginity! Tonight! It's going to feel heavenly...like the other day on the couch times a million.

I look out the window and watch as the snows falls, melting when it hits the street. I start writing a song about it in my head.

*

Amy has whiskey in the kitchen. I've never drank much before, beyond a little wine. The shot is disgusting as I throw it back, but immediately, the veins in my temples surge with pleasurable heat, and the warmth spreads throughout my body. Amy takes a second shot then pours some in a glass for us to share.

C'mere, she says, and she takes both my hands, placing them on her waist. I lower my chin, blushing. She holds the glass of ice and whiskey beneath my nose. It smells terrible, but I take it and gulp some down. Amy takes it back from my hand.

Follow me, she says. She leads me up the stairs in the dark, still holding my right hand. I stumble a little, giggling, but I don't fall. I wonder where her mom and step-dad are tonight. Work, probably. I wonder how late it is.

Amy turns on the television in her room. TMT is showing some old movie from the 1950's. I don't recognize it. There's a guy in a red jacket—he's in a car race I'm pretty sure. Amy mutes it as she lies down on her back. She pulls me down on top of her and wraps her legs around me. We don't kiss. Not on the mouth at least. She's biting and sucking my neck, I think. It's hard to tell what's happening because my head is so hot with booze. I roll off to my right and lay on my back. My breaths feel shallow and coated with a film. Gimme a sec.

Amy sighs, sounding frustrated. She sits up and lifts the whiskey glass from the bed stand. She holds it out towards me.

I clear my throat. I dunno, I say. I'm good.

It'll be fine. Just have a little more to loosen up.

I sit up and sip a little. She tilts the glass, and I swallow more. I feel like I'm going to vomit and I cover my mouth. I see her face through the bottom of the glass and I feel happy. Then I feel nothing.

~ ~ ~

I open my eyes and see the television. The guy in the red jacket is smoking a cigarette. His head is in the girl's lap. He's pretty. I try to ask Amy who he is, but all that comes out is a strained sort of noise. She pulls me closer to her, on my side. She's topless. She pushes my head down to her breasts. Yes...this is nice. It's warm. I want to sleep here. Good night.

She rolls me back onto my back. Now she's leaning over me. Why can't she let me sleep? She's shaking my shoulder and saying my name. What? Why?

I open my eyes again. Woo, guess I dozed off there for a second.

My pants are off. Her hand is in my underwear. But I'm too drunk and I can't feel it.

Please?

No. No, I don't want this, not yet, not now, not if I can't feel it. Let's just cuddle. Let's just focus on her boobs and sleeping—pillows. I try to lift my hand, to grab her hand, to stop her, but I don't know how. It isn't working. My arm I mean. My arm isn't working.

Shhh, she says, it's OK.

But it isn't OK. I look at the TV. I'm slipping away. It isn't OK. It isn't OK.

~ ~ ~

I wake as a sharp pain shoots through my lower abdomen. Her finger's where I tried to put a tampon once, but it hurt and I gave up and forgot about it after that. It feels similar—that stabbing pain, below my belly. Ow, fuck. She's scratching me with her nails. She's scratching out my insides.

Stop! Voice? Where is my voice? It isn't in my throat. The sound is coming out somewhere else, far away, and no one can hear it. I wish I could make her stop. It's un*com*fortable. Is this sex? There must be something wrong with me because this is awful. I want to make her stop but I can't. I can't focus, and it's easier to just close my eyes. Easier just to wait. If I try to move I might fall off the bed. She might hate me. I'm too dizzy. Why doesn't she just rub, like before? Why is she clawing at me like that? What's she trying to find? At least I am close to her. At least this means she likes me. It's best if I just lie still and wait til it's over. I can do this. I can get through this.

~ ~ ~

I open my eyes. She stopped. My shirt and three sports bras are off, somehow. What time is it? I realize Amy is behind me, propping me up from behind. How does this work? She's stroking my chest. I hate my chest. Please. Don't ...

80

But I can't tell her that. I don't want be alone when boys throw shit and yell *dyke*. I can't see anything but my body in front of me. Are we on the couch? How did we get here? Where did my clothes go? I feel gross and exposed. I'm so pale. My nipples are small and pink and awkwardly soft. The snow in the window reflects a white, chilly light on my body. Where is that light coming from? The glow of the TV is blue, but this light is white. I have a headache. I can't hold off sleep any longer.

~ ~ ~

Your chest is like a boys, Amy says. I don't understand how she can talk, because I still can't focus enough to think. She sounds far away. It takes a minute for my vision to stop blurring, and the room spins.

How..? I don't know what I'm trying to say.

You look like James Dean, she says, if I put your hair like this. It's cute.

I feel a surge of pride over the nauseated confusion. I'm a boy! Wait.

~ ~ ~

Black. Unconsciousness is black, and so is semi-consciousness. Are your dreams in black and white? How can you remember? How can anyone remember anything with these long blackouts in between? Even the unfettered mind sleeps, and forgets everything, second by second, with each blink. Death wipes what's left away.

~ ~ ~

I open my eyes and see her smiling at me.

You're probably a boy inside, she says.

Inside.

Well, yeah, of course?

Even though I'm too drunk to agree, Amy nods knowingly. Yeah, you're definitely a transgender. Have you heard of that? She plays with my hair, and I begin to relax a little. It feels good. I'm a transgender. I'm James Dean. I'm not sure who that is, but I know it's a good thing. She sculpts it into a point...a pompadour of sorts.

You should wear it like this, she says. It's more masculine. You'll pass as a guy that way.

OK, I manage to mumble.

And you need a different name. A boy's name. She looks at me with those wintery blue eyes.

I love you, I think.

She smiles. I'm going to call you Dean, she says.

Dykes

Amy starts dating Morgan again. It's been less than a week since we did what we did. To make matters even more baffling, Morgan is being sent to Catholic school. Her parents are concerned about the influence of the public school environment (ie. Amy). Why does Amy want to date someone who won't be around? So far, all they do is hold one another and cry all the time. I don't get it.

I feel dirty. I've stopped eating pretty much all together. I'll have toast two or three times a day, but that's about it. I don't think my stomach can handle anything else. I don't sleep much either. I always wake up around 4 or 5 AM, only hours after I finally drift off to sleep. I zone out during classes and sleep at lunch. When I get home, I sleep some more. My body is always achy, tight, and cold. Every muscles feels like a taught rubber band, ready to snap. I feel a little nuts, to be honest.

Between class periods, I stop to drop off my books at my locker. I feel a hand on my waist and I spin around, nearly slugging Amy by mistake. Every little thing startles me lately—a touch, a slamming door, a dropped book, a telephone ringing...

Amy grabs my face and kisses me, just as a group of guys walk by. I'm too surprised to react.

Dykes! The boys stop, jeering and leering.

I'll turn you straight. One's grabbing his junk and looking at Amy. He has his hand down his sweatpants. It's the boy who bothered me in the art room. I can see the outline of his dick.

The others laugh. Suck on this, bitch.

Fuck off, I say, giving him the finger.

Oh hell no! Bitch you don't say that to me. I'll put a bag over your head and fuck you too. If you even got a pussy.

They all laugh.

Amy pins me against the locker.

What are you doing?

Kiss me, she says.

They'll just harass us more, I say. Other people are gathering too, and the halls are filled with students.

Who cares what they think? Amy whispers. Just kiss me.

I…I can't. I'm blushing furiously. I don't want to Amy.

She sighs and kisses me instead. I want to pull away but I can feel the anger in her body as it presses against me. If I pull away, she'll turn on me.

The jocks are watching intently now. She takes my hand in hers and raises it to her lips. She looks right at the guys and slips my pointer and index finger between her lips, sucking on them as she pulls them out. I look at the floor, ashamed.

Nice, one of the boys says. I notice several of them have placed their binders or textbooks in front of their crotches.

The bell rings, and everyone walks away. I open my locker and just stare into it, with no concept of the time that is passing, until one of the deans finds me and writes me up for cutting class.

The Soprano Section

Oh Christ and now we're in Chorus class. We're sitting in chairs, in rows, watching a movie in the dark. We always watch movies in this class. Amy passes me a dirty note. I feel nauseated. I write back: What about Morgan?

If you don't do it I'll find someone else, Amy writes. When I look over at her, I'm startled to see that she's crying. I sigh. I move as quietly as possible over a few chairs to her section—the sopranos. She motions for me to move the chair even closer, so I do.

She wipes away her tears and drapes her sweatshirt over her lap. She takes my hand and puts it in her pocket. I know the routine—she's cut out the pockets. She urges my fingers toward her *you-know-what*. I close my eyes. I feel humiliated, and I literally pray to God, silently, that no one is watching me. What if it gets back to my mother? I remember how it felt when Amy did this to me, and my body shivers.

But what's worse is, against my will, I'm aroused. How can that be? I must actually want to. I'm just scared.

She pushes on my fingers through her fabric of her pants so that the tip of my right pointer enters her. She nods.

It's warm and wet. I swallow and then begin to move my fingers in and out slowly. Soon I've worked up to my knuckle.

She's biting on her hand. Use two, she mouths.

I maneuver my middle finger in as well and keep pushing them in and out. I'm scared, disgusted, and burning with desire all at once.

I wish you had bigger fingers, she whispers. Like Morgan's.

I just stare at my lap.

Hey! the teacher shouts at me.

I jump. What?

I told you a million times: stay in your own section!

I pull my fingers out as quickly as possible and cross my hands in my lap. I'm sorry.

She fills out a yellow slip and sends me to the dean.

Twice in one week? the dean says. He sends me to ISS.

ISS is in-school suspension. You spend the whole day in a classroom with no windows, no talking, and no lunch break. I'm there the rest of the week.

Toxic

We need to talk, my mom says one day when I get home from school.

What?

I found this. She is holding my red notebook.

What the hell! Did you read my journal?

Only because I'm worried.

That's not fair! It's private!

Then you shouldn't have written it down, she says. She's been saying that since I was a kid. Never write down anything you don't want to be read. Easy for her to say.

Give it to me!

No, she says. Listen to me.

She sits me down at the kitchen table. You aren't allowed at Amy's house anymore.

What! That's not fair!

And you aren't allowed to spend time with her outside of school. If you have to for some reason, an adult has to supervise.

You can't tell me what to do!

I'm trying to help you. You'll thank me one day.

No I won't.

I feel like I'm losing you. She's brainwashing you.

No she isn't! How pathetic do you think I am?

It's not that you're pathetic. She manipulates you.

You don't even know her! God, just leave me alone. It's my life.

But I'm your mother and it's my job to look after you. Amy is toxic.

What does that even mean?

I call Amy to tell her the bad news. She isn't responsive.

Are you mad at me? I ask.

She doesn't respond. I broke up with Morgan, she says.

I silently pump my fist. Oh how come?

She said I raped her.

What? I snort.

She just doesn't want to admit she's a lesbian, Amy says. She says she's straight now.

Wow, I say. That's messed up

Becoming Dean

After winter break, some of our classes switch. In my art class, I sit next to a girl named Vivian and I start to develop a little crush on her.

There isn't much hope with Vivian because she's straight. But there isn't much hope with Amy either. I hoped she would ask me out now that she's single, but she's taken the opportunity instead to mess around with all the willing girls in the school. Despite myself, I hope that Vivian might like me back, if I get up the nerve to tell her my secret.

Amy was right about one thing—I'm transgender. I've started researching it during lunch on the school computers. I start by typing "transgender female" which takes me to Wikipedia. I find out that this is called "FTM" or "female-to-male." I try typing that into the search bar. Many of the sites are blocked, but I manage to get through to one called Hudson's FTM Resource Guide.

"In FTM testosterone therapy, testosterone (often called "T" for short) can be administered into the body in a number of ways. The most common method is intramuscular injection with a syringe."

I'll have to get over my fear of needles.

"Over time, the ongoing administration of testosterone will result in the development of masculine secondary sex characteristics, as well as the cessation of menses (monthly periods)."

Thank God.

"The following masculinizing effects can be

expected as a result of testosterone therapy. These effects may take several months to be noticeable, and will continue to develop over a period of years.

- Thickening of the vocal chords and deepening of the voice
- Facial hair growth (mustache and/or beard growth)
- Increased body hair growth (notably on arms, legs, chest, belly, and back)
- Increased body musculature
- Enlargement of the clitoris
- Cessation of menses (monthly periods)
- Potential hair loss at the temples and crown of the head, resulting in a more masculine hairline; possibly male-pattern baldness
- Migration of body fat to a more masculine pattern (i.e., fat deposits shifting from hips, thighs and buttocks to the abdomen area)
- Increased activity of the skin's oil glands (i.e., skin becomes more oily, which may result in acne)
- Scent of body odors and urine may change
- Skin may become rougher in feeling and/or appearance.
- Increase in sex drive "

Well most of that sounds positive! Admittedly, I don't want to be bald…and I'm not sure what a clitoris is. Everything else sounds almost too good to be true. Could I really live my life as a man?

I type in "FTM before and after pictures." Some of these men are actually attractive. I would have never known their pasts.

I type "clitoris" into Google, but it's blocked and a red page pops up, warning me that any more violations will result in the suspension of my account. I guess I'll have to find an actual dictionary somewhere. You think there'd be more available—we *are* in a school.

After lunch means back to art class. We're working on clay pots, and this is one art form in which I have no skill. Vivian laughs as I lump more clay onto my already lumpy vessel. Hers is damn near perfect. Most everything she does is perfect. She's also in my Honors English class, and she's the smartest student. She's gorgeous, but no guys really notice her because she's heavy. She's around 5'4, and I have no idea what weight because I'm horrible at estimating those things. 200 pounds, my mom estimated once over dinner, telling my dad about my new friend. I thought it was rude and irrelevant. Still, Mom's happy I'm hanging out with anyone who isn't Amy.

You're such a mess, Vivian says affectionately as I fumble with the tools. Look at your clothes.

In addition to already being speckled with paint, my cut-off jeans are now caked with clay.

It's matted in your leg hair! Vivian squeals. She's the first person I've met, including Amy, that isn't bothered by the fact that I stopped shaving.

It'd be weird with most girls, she said once, But you're not really a girl. Not really.

That's when I decided I was falling for her. She's got shoulder-length dark hair and light green eyes. She's a quarter Armenian, a quarter Dutch, and half Italian. She wears black-framed glasses that no one realizes are awesome because no one around here has any sense of style. Vivian does. And she likes indie music. Vivian is quite literally too cool for school.

And she reads books! Her favorite author is F. Scott Fitzgerald, who I haven't read, but I'll get to it eventually. Amy likes to pretend she reads books, but she doesn't really. She carries *Thus Spoke Zarathustra* under her arm all the time, but I don't think she actually understands any of it. I paged through it one day and it was pretty much crap. Really hard to understand, so that it sounds deep and philosophical. Kinda like Amy actually. "God is dead, oooh." Give me a break.

Strangely, I'm being harassed more than ever. Amy has stopped spending time with me and you'd think people would leave me alone for being a so-called dyke. I think I'm just an even easier target on my own. The worst culprit is this gay guy named Matt Wilson. He's never actually told anyone he's gay, but it's obvious. There are lots of rumors about him too, such as that he's actually way older than the rest of us and failed ninth grade twice. He's a stoner, with piercings all over his face and bleached blonde hair. He sleeps with older men for drugs and money, some people say. I don't understand why he and his trashy straight girl friends have singled me out. They follow me in the hall, calling me names and throwing things at me. One day at lunch, they have a pack of condoms. They stretch them and put them onto bananas, acting like it's the most hilarious thing in the world. Grow up already.

Hey I bet you wish you had one of these! Matt shouts at me, meaning a banana. Meaning a dick. I just roll my eyes. Yeah I bet you wish you did, too.

When everyone is leaving the cafeteria, each of them takes a turn pelting me with a condom-covered banana or two. One hits me in the back of the head. There are a couple teachers in the hall, and I know they saw what happened, but they don't do anything. Nobody cares. I believe in the power of Civil Disobedience, so I refuse to fight back, even when one girl shoves me from behind and I fall on the floor.

Dyke!

I don't tell Vivian about any of this. I don't want to scare her away. My other friends like Gabe and Benny are harassed sometimes too, but not as much—only in gym. Gabe got shoved in a locker, and people call him a chink...but people generally don't mind Benny because he's in the closet. He doesn't flaunt his gayness, the way Gabe and I supposedly do. Forget the fact that I never actually said I was gay. It's not about that, really. It's about the way I dress—the person I really am. It's about Dean.

I've decided I like that name. I rented *Rebel Without a Cause* from the library and watched it with my mom. I liked it alright, but I was mostly just interested in James Dean as a person. I checked out some biographies of him as well. He was a pretty depressed guy and I relate to him a lot. The books are full of pictures. I begin to fill my wardrobe with Levis and black tees from the Salvation Army. I even buy some gold hair dye at the drug store and manage to do an all right job streaking it through my hair. I trim it even shorter so that my ears show. I get it to stick up by brushing it back while it's still wet. Soon it does it automatically. I'm too scrawny and feminine, but if I blur my eyes, my reflection almost resembles him. I feel confident.

The new look seems to work magic. I walk through the halls without drawing attention to myself. Who would have thought? I make it to art class unscathed. I sit down next to Vivian, who is busy at work with the clay. I say something and she is startled.

You look so different. Like a guy! I mean you always did, but now you *really* do.

She's blushing. I'm beaming. I know it's only a matter of time until people start recognizing me again—and they do. But strangely, no one seems to care anymore. I pass through like a ghost among the kids in my grade, and the younger ones all seem to think I'm a guy. The only time I do get harassed, it's by some boys in my neighborhood who call me a fag and try to push me off my bike. I narrowly escape, but I'm just happy that I passed. Winter turns to spring, and soon school lets out for the summer. Finally, I am done at the junior high school for good. Perhaps the high school will provide a much-needed Amy-free fresh start.

Fourth of July

Gabe invites us to his parents' house on the fourth of July. "Us" is comprised of me, Benny, Vivian, and Amy. Gabe lives on the lake, out in Cicero—that's a suburb to the north. We spend much of the afternoon wading in the water, gazing out at the small wooded islands. We decided that when Gabe's parents retire and move away, we'll all live here in this house. It's not just the view—inside there is a spiral staircase, fish tank, and large screen television.

Amy keeps holding my hand. I'm embarrassed when Gabe's mom or dad is around because I know they are conservative. They accept that Gabe is gay, but I'm pretty sure they feel all same-sex affection should be kept private. I can't say I disagree—I hate that Amy makes me do this shit. But I'm happy she is paying attention to me again. The summer is off to a good start. I have hope that we might end up dating for real this time.

We eat a pizza dinner at a wooden picnic table with a checkered tablecloth. It's summer and will be hours before the sun begins to set. We've doused ourselves with mosquito repellant, but we're still getting dive-bombed by the wretched things. Gabe's parents are inside, so I decide it's a good time to bring up the transgender subject—at least as good as any. All day I've been wincing at the sound of my name and the use of female pronouns. It's not that I ever liked it, but now that I know there's an alternative, it's downright intolerable.

What would you guys say if...I told you... I think I'm a boy? I mean, I don't think. I know I am. I'm a boy.

There's a few moment of silence.

Vivian is the first person to speak. That makes sense, she says.

Gabe nods in agreement. Do you mean you want to get a sex change or something?

Sort of. I want to go by a different name, and by *he* and *him*. I've been reading online about people that take hormones and they basically changed into men.

Benny looks skeptical. So you just take a pill and grow a penis?

No, I say, a little crestfallen. Your voice gets lower, you grow a beard...

But you still have a vagina, Benny says.

That's none of you're business, I say.

I think you'd be sexy with a beard. Gabe winks at me. I laugh.

Benny looks uncomfortable.

What name do you want to go by? Vivian asks.

Dean, Amy says. Like James Dean.

That's perfect for you, Gabe says. Damn, I wish I could change my name! Gabe is a weird name for an Asian.

What would you change it to? I ask.

Ignacio, Gabe says, without hesitation.

Of course, I say.

I have an idea! Gabe says, slapping his palms on the tablecloth. We should give Dean a makeover!

I pretend to be annoyed as the girls and Gabe fuss over my appearance. They darken my eyebrows and wispy sideburns with brown mascara. Gabe is good with makeup, so he uses it to highlight my more masculine facial features, like my cheekbones and jaw line. Then he gets his tuxedo out of the closet.

Wear this! he says

I go into the bathroom to change. I put the billowing white dress shirt on over my white tee and tuck it into the black pants. I wrap the cumberbun around my waist. Gabe is small like me, so it all fits pretty well, including the polished black shoes. For some reason, I'm nervous to look in the mirror. I always dress like a boy, kind of. But this feels different. This feels more real, and more frightening. I'm not sure there's any going back.

Come out already! Gabe says, We want to see how you look!

Speak for yourself, Benny mumbles.

I step awkwardly out of the bathroom, clinging to the doorframe.

Oh my god, Vivian says. She's blushing.

You look so hot! Gabe says.

Back off, Amy says, He's mine.

It's hard to tell if she's joking, and Vivian looks a little affronted. I don't care though. I'm Amy's? Really?

Take a look at yourself! Gabe says, turning me around towards the mirror. I grin.

Route 11 at Night by Bicycle

It's a cool, windy night in August—about 11:30 or so. I ride my bike down Allen Road in the dark. To say I snuck out of the house seems dramatic. True, my parents are asleep and don't know that I'm going. But does it matter? I'm sixteen.

I shouldn't be biking on the main roads, but there aren't any cars so I figure I'm fine. It's a weeknight and no one's really out this late. I pass a neon red sign for Arby's Roast Beef in the shape of a huge cowboy hat, Gino and Joe's Pizza, and the huge McDonalds arch. I pass stoplights, auto shops, and eventually the strip mall. The lights make everything look like a small, squashed city—a miniature Tokyo or New York, at least what I've seen of them in pictures. Suburbs sprawl around the main strip. The roads merge, and I turn left. A right turn would take me to the highway and then to the city. I glide under the overpass. A man killed himself earlier this summer by jumping off this stone block bridge onto the highway below.

Thunder cracks in the distance. The wind whips with more fervor. It's going to storm soon. Just my luck. It starts to rain as I turn onto Amy's street. I'm surprised how short of a journey it is between our neighboring towns.

I'm drenched as I chain my bike to the lamppost. I let myself into the entranceway and rap my aching, cold knuckles on the door. Amy answers.

Oh God Dean! You're soaked to the bone.

Soothing, motherly words. I wish she were always like this. I wish this was our house in the suburbs and that we were ten years older. No one else is home, as usual, so I can pretend this is our own house.

Amy leads me upstairs, and I am caught off guard by blurry memories of whiskey and the night I lost my virginity. My stomach turns sour and I struggle to maintain the warm feeling I felt in the entranceway. Still, I need to be taken care of. I need my body to be loved. It's beyond a physical need.

My clothes come off. I'm cold and wet. Will she put them in the dryer? Yes, she takes them downstairs. I'm alone for a few minutes. I stand naked in the dark, shivering. I wish I had a towel. My b-r-e-a-s-t-s are so cold they are almost purple. The n-i-p-p-l-e-s are hard. I barely look, but I know. Sometimes when my skin is cold enough, there are orange specks in the purple. My hands are bloodless. Poor circulation is in my genes.

Amy's back and we lay in the bed. She starts right at it, doing it to me. I have trouble keeping my legs spread. It hurts, but that's just the way it goes. I can't help thinking about what Benny said. I can't help thinking this would be easier if I had a penis. She's kneeling and leaning over me now, still doing it. I keep my eyes on the walls. They're turquoise blue. There's no light except what comes through the blinds. A streetlamp, maybe. It's a pale white glow. There's a wind chime made of seashells, but the window is closed, so it stays silent and motionless. It's a beautifully sad room.

Amy whispers, I like the way your face screws up...like you're in pain.

I smile weakly. I'm barely listening. I let my mind wander. I'm thinking about the ocean and the wind. I remember when Amy said I was the wind. I remember when she brought me a seashell from Cancun. It had my old name written on it. I remember when I wrote "Dean +Amy" in a heart in the sand. I was on the shore of Lake Ontario—the fake ocean, Mom called it. The waves washed it away in three cycles. The power plant in the distance gave the lake away as nothing but a lake.

After Amy's done, I put on my dry clothes and I ride my bike home. It hurts a little to sit. There must be something wrong with me down there because it always hurts, even when I try to do it myself. I only like it if I rub. You see, I sort of have a tiny penis. I've since I was a kid, but I never really thought about it again until I started having sex. I think I might be a hermaphrodite—that would explain a lot. I wonder if Amy noticed.

It's stopped raining but the mud on the road splatters up and onto my back as I ride. My hands are still cold. The sun is rising as I turn onto my street and then up the driveway to park my bike in the garage. After that, I sit on the stone porch. I don't know why, but I can't stop crying.

It's Gross

Amy and I sneak out of school in the early afternoon. It's beautiful outside—May is always my favorite time of year. We cross the road and find a field. There are pine trees creating a grove, and we nestle down beside it, making a nest of sorts in the tall grass.

I undress her tenderly. After all this time I'm still unsure. Is this OK? What about this? Can I kiss you here? I know that if I do something wrong I could lose her forever.

I don't finger her. She just wants me to stroke the opening. I do this for awhile as her breathing grows heavy. She's shaved bare, as usual, beneath her short plaid skirt. She isn't wearing a bra beneath her ribbed tank top either. I lift it up and I kiss her breasts. In the daylight, I notice how big and puffy her nipples are. I put my mouth on one. She moans softly and grips at my hair. I push my fingers into her, still sucking on her nipple. She gasps, then comes, hard and trembling, her vagina pulsing around my fingers.

I lay beside her as she catches her breath. I shield the sun from my eyes with my hand. The spaces between my fingers glow with a red aura in the light. I'm aroused enough that I think I might come if she tried.

I nudge her, smiling goofily.

What, she says.

I blush and shrug.

She sits up and reaches for her bag. We should get going.

But…what about me?

You?

Yeah.

She sighs, not sad but impatient. I can't. I don't like to anymore.

What do you mean? You do it all the time.

I know and...I realized it's gross. I like boys now.

This is a low blow, and I feel the effects on my body more than my mind. It's almost as if the wind's been knocked out of me. My chest feels like someone is pressing on it, trying to cause it to cave.

I guess I'm straight, she says.

But I'm a boy. The words are small and insecure, almost a question.

She looks at me with what can only be described as pity. You aren't really though; you just went along with what I said...and I shouldn't have said that. She half-smiles. I just want you to be you.

No, I am! I'm a boy I mean. I've always been, you just offered me an out—an opportunity. When you said I was transgender, I just was finally able to admit it. I had the words for it.

She shakes her head. Well even if so, you're not an actual guy.

What's the difference? I wish I hadn't asked.

I told you, she said, pointing, I find it gross.

I bury my face in my hands. How do you know though? I say, emerging, How do you know if you've never been with a guy?

She doesn't answer.

I sigh. Have you?

Yeah. She's talking like a little girl. A quiet, stupid baby.

Speak up! I say, even though I heard. Why don't you ever speak the fuck up?

Yeah, she says. My neighbor. I gave head to my neighbor.

Oh that's just great, I say, laughing. Excellent. Good to know.

Blue Pills

I take the late bus home. I'm one of the only people onboard. I'm not even sure what happened to Amy and whether she got a ride or not. I don't really care.

I get off early at Main Street and Chestnut, a couple miles from my house. It's around 4:30, and there aren't yet that many cars on the road. Main Street is where Rt. 11 transverses the village of North Syracuse. In the 1800's it was called Plank Road, because it was made of wooden planks three inches thick and eight feet long. It was the first plank road in America, made to transport salt.

Now there's just a regular asphalt road, covered with potholes, with double painted yellow lines down it. It's trying to pose as a small town, with all the American flags. There's a little barbershop, a florist, and a veterans memorial made of bricks, listing names of the dead carved in stone. None of the buildings are that tall—most are only one story. Behind the strip of businesses are small houses built in the 50's, with unkempt yards and rusted cars with FOR SALE signs in the windows.

I cross the street, glancing at St. Rose as I walk past. Down the street further is the Baptist church, with its huge steeple and Death Star-like windows. There is a huge, fake bible in the yard, open to a page that reads, *Jesus said: I am the way, the truth, the light. Him that cometh to me I will no wise cast out.*

Lies.

I walk through the black iron gates into North Syracuse cemetery. The grass surrounding the graves is green and healthy from the spring showers. It's a small cemetery, compared to the ones in the city. Some of those are like their own towns, with statues and masoleums. Here there are only graves—some tall and phallic, others simple stone markers. The limestone has been weathered away on much of the 19th century gravestones, but they still are more attractive than the new graves, with their artificial luster that brings to mind a countertop.

I sit down in the shade, under a tree. I've been crying the whole way since I left Amy and the high school. I unzip the front pocket of my backpack and I find a plastic baggy of pills that I haven't been taking—the ADD medication. I also have a water bottle in my backpack with a little bit of water left. I swallow them all in one gulp. Then I lie down in the grass and close my eyes.

Soon I feel elation. I am confident in the decision I've made, and I know that whether I die or not, this was meant to be. Everything I do is predestined and perfect. A bee lands on my arm. I watch it do bee things.

I hear voices—mostly girls. By the gate I see Vivian, Gabe, Benny, and a bunch of girls with trash bags. They are members of a club that cleans up the neighborhoods. It's supposed to help them get into colleges someday.

They're coming into the cemetery. Vivian sees me and furrows her brow as she hastens her pace. The others follow her.

"Hi," I say when she has arrived at my side. "I might need some help."

Saint Joseph's Hospital

I lie in the hospital bed, facing the wall. I wish my parents weren't here. It's embarrassing. I can't tell how long since my father arrived—mom rode with me in the ambulance.

I can't remember much of anything, to be honest with you. A male nurse gave me a concoction of charcoal and Capri Sun. He told me to try my hardest not to puke it up, or they'd have to pump the poison out of my stomach. I didn't know what that meant, but it sounded painful. The drink tasted terrible and made me gag.

I can remember peeing in a bedpan. My pants were off, so everyone could see me. I was humiliated, but I needed to go. The room was spinning. Someone must have stuck IVs in my arms at some point. I remember the beeping of the heart monitor. I blacked out.

You're lucky you made it, a nurse says. Your heart rate was dangerously high.

She points to the bandages on my arms. The IVs left bruises, because your blood pressure was so high.

After she leaves, I tell Mom and Dad, without looking at them, that I'm sorry and I learned my lesson and no, I didn't really want to die, it was just a cry for help, although I'm not sure whether that's true.

Everything's fine now, I say several times. But they are still really upset and crying. I feel horrible and I cry, too.

By the time we leave the hospital it's about midnight. I passed the psychological test (Are you going to harm yourself again? Are you going to harm anyone else?) so they aren't going to lock me away

107

like in the movies. I'm back in my clothes, and we walk to the car. I insisted I didn't need a wheelchair.

Everything's fine now, I say again. I feel strangely hyper. We're in the city, and I realize it was Saint Joseph's, the same hospital where I was born and where Dad works. Saint Joseph was Jesus' dad—the guy in the manger.

For an urban environment, everything is strangely still. The streets are wide and cracked, the streetlights are out, and the red brick buildings are abandoned or for rent. When we get to the car, Dad locks the doors right away. A train sounds in the distance.

At home, I can't sleep. I decide to move everything from my old bedroom into the guest room, and visa versa. I suspect that I would have never been able to sleep in my bedroom again. Mom sees what I'm doing, but she doesn't try to stop me. She just makes me keep the door open.

The guest room is tiny, but I find that comforting. Soon, I'm exhausted. My cat Brownie comes in and cuddles with me in bed. As we fall asleep, I think about the real reason I swallowed the pills. I decide that I need to transition from female to male. I need to start taking hormones as soon as possible, and I can't let anything stop me.

That night I dream about Grandma for the first time in years. She tells me she knows I'm transgender, and she still loves me anyway.

The Plan

I don't go back to school the next week, both because I am recovering and because they suspended me for drug possession. It isn't long until the semester ends anyway. I go in to take my finals and that's it. I don't see Amy and my mom won't let me call her.

I fail my Math exam, so I have to go to summer school. I use that time to make a plan.

Step 1: find a psychiatrist

I need a letter from a therapist, diagnosing me with Gender Identity Disorder, in order to start injecting testosterone. I found this out on Hudson's FTM Resource Guide.

Step 2: Get someone to drive me to therapist
Step 3: Attend 15 sessions and get a letter
Step 4: Find an endocrinologist
Step 5: Get Rx for testosterone, using savings
Step 6: Find a job to fund testosterone
Step 7: Start saving for chest surgery

I'm already being forced to see a therapist, due to the fact that I tried to kill myself in May. I'm not sure if she'll be cool with the idea, but I don't know anyone else to ask. She is the same shrink that prescribed me ADD medicine. Now she has me on anti-depressants, because she is pretty sure she misread my situation.

Telling someone you are transgender is next to impossible. I have no idea how to bring it up. So far, I've told her very little about myself, because I don't trust her at all. She probably reports back to my parents everything I say.

Have you ever heard of transgender? I ask.

Yes, why?

I think—no, I know—that I am transgender.

She doesn't seem surprised. She somewhat reluctantly gives me the phone number of a support group. She doesn't know when or where they meet, because they only tell you if you call ahead, for safety purposes.

Despite my fear of phones, I call the number that same evening.

Hello? A man says

Hello. Do you hold, uh, meetings?

What kind of meetings?

Oh. Uh…never mind.

No, no! We do have meetings. Were you looking for the support group?

Yes, I say, The one about…gender.

We meet every Thursday at 5 at the ACR building. Do you know where that is?

No, I say.

How old are you?

18, I say, which is a lie.

It's 444 East Genesee Street, he says.

Oh OK, I say, as if I have any idea where that is.

I can't tell my parents. That is absolutely out of the question. I already put them through enough with trying to kill myself and all. Besides, I know what my mom will say—that I'm just doing it because of Amy. And then if she found out Amy liked guys now, she'd believe it even more.

But something has changed. I don't care about Amy anymore. Gabe told me she was dating her neighbor now—that guy she gave a blowjob. It hurt to hear, but I was able to let it go. I have more important things to worry about. Perhaps it was the near death experience, or perhaps it's turning sixteen. It just doesn't seem like a big deal anymore. I have Gabriel, Vivian, and Benny. I have my art, music, and writing.

Maybe I'll tell Mom after I raise my grades next year. I realized I have to get into college. I can't be transgender and live in Syracuse. People are too hateful here. I have to get away.

I plan on going to the meeting next week and finding out how this whole transgender thing works. If I find a psychiatrist, I can start going to my sessions and hopefully I'll get a letter saying I can start hormones. In less than two years, I'll be 18 and heading to college. Then I will be on my own and able to do as I please. I can start over someplace new, as a boy. As Dean.

I was thinking about choosing a different name— because, you know, Amy gave it to me, and I'm trying to move on. But the funny thing is, it's become a part of me now. I can't imagine being anyone else.

About the Author

Elliott Lawrence Renehan DeLine (born 1988) is a novelist, short story writer, and essayist from Syracuse, NY. He graduated from Syracuse University in 2012 with a BA in English. His first book, *Refuse,* was a finalist in the 2011 LGBT Rainbow Awards. His work has been featured in several publications, including *The Collection,* a finalist for the 2012 Lambda Literary Awards. He currently lives with his family and cat in North Syracuse, New York. He spends most his time in the city of Syracuse, Instagram-ing derelict buildings, typing in libraries, and single-handedly supporting the local coffee shops with his patronage.

For more information, please visit
elliottdelineofficial.wordpress.com

Follow Elliott DeLine on the web at
elliottdeline.tumblr.com
@elliottdeline
fb.com/authorelliottdeline

Also By Elliott DeLine ...Dean's college years

Available online in paperback and various ebook
formats. **Visit elliottdelineofficial.wordpress.com/refuse**

"*Refuse* is a stunning debut "novoir" about an over-
observant young outsider with really great hair who is
outside everything – including the transgender community
– but keeps a great deal bottled up inside. Funny, cynical,
tough, vulnerable, honest, deluded, sagacious, self-loving
and self-loathing, *Refuse* is irresistible."
Mark Simpson, author of *Saint Morrissey*

"Elliott DeLine is an ambitious, witty, self-deprecating,
thoughtful writer whose debut novel Refuse could
meaningfully be compared to the work of Dennis Cooper
(with far less violence), Brett Easton Ellis (with far fewer
chemical substances), David Sedaris (with not as many
belly laughs) and Leslie Feinberg (with a much less
mournful air)...With this as his debut effort, DeLine, not
yet out of college, is a writer to watch."
Out in Print Queer Book Reviews

47727538R00071

Made in the USA
Middletown, DE
31 August 2017